ORDINARY DAY
A Novel of 9/11

BY J.R. REILING

American Airlines Flight #11

BOEING 767

ZONE A - FIRST
9 SEATS

ZONE B - BUSINESS
30 SEATS

ZONE C - ECONOMY
119 SEATS

SEAT	PASSENGER
10B	Al Suqami, Satam
34C	Allison, Anna
8G	Alomari, Abdul
2A	Alshehri, Wail
2B	Alshehri, Waleed
8A	Angell, David
8B	Angell, Lynn Edwards
29C	Aoyama, Selma
	Arestegui, Barbara
28C	Aronson, Myra
8D	Atta, Mohamed
25C	Barbuto, Christine
11D	Beug, Carolyn
26G	Booms, Kelly
3B	Bouchard, Carol
33H	Casey, Nellie
	Collman, Jeffrey
20H	Coombs, Jeffrey
33J	Creamer, Tara

SEAT	PASSENGER
27J	Cuccinello, Thelma
10U	Curnivan, Patrick
25U	Dale, Brian
27A	DiMeglio, David
23B	DiTullio, Donald
11U	Domínguez, Alberto
7A	Farley-Hackel, Paige
22U	Filipov, Alexander
3H	Flyzik, Carol
28H	Friedman, Paul
20U	Fyfe, Karleton
9H	Gay, Peter
28J	George, Linda
9A	Glazer, Edmund
32H	Gordenstein, Lisa
11A	Green, Andrew
20A	Hashem, Peter
9J	Hayes, Robert

SEAT	PASSENGER
10A	Hennessy, Jr., Edward
24J	Hofer, John
27H	Holland, Cora
22A	Humber, Jr., John N.
31A	Iskandar, Waleed
3U	Jenkins, John
31G	Jones, Charles
22H	Kaplan, Robin
19B	Keating, Barbara
20B	Kovalcin, David
26J	Larocque, Judith C.
23A	Lasden, Natalie Janis
31J	Lee, Daniel
9B	Lewin, Daniel
	Low, Sara
32J	Mackay, Susan
	Martin, Karen
	McGuinness, Jr., Thomas

SEAT	PASSENGER
11B	Mello, Christopher
11H	Mladenik, Jeffrey
23H	Montoya, Carlos
2D	Morabito, Laura
24B	Naiman, Mildred
28B	Neira, Laurie
3A	Newell, Renee
	Nicosia, Kathleen
27B	Norton, Jacqueline
27C	Norton, Robert
	Ogonowski, John
	Ong, Betty
31B	Orth, Jane
28J	Pecorelli, Thomas
19A	Perkins, Berinthia
3J	Puopolo, Sonia
2H	Retik, David
	Rogér, Jean

SEAT	PASSENGER
11G	Rosenzweig, Philip
2J	Ross, Richard
22B	Sachs, Jessica
35G	Salie, Rahma
26B	Smith, Heather
	Snyder, Dianne
25B	Stone, Douglas
34J	Suarez, Xavier
	Sweeney, Madeline
35C	Theodoridis, Michael
30A	Trentini, James
30B	Trentini, Mary Barbara
22J	Valdes, Antonio Montoya
36J	Vamsikrishna, Pendyala
10H	Wahlstrom, Mary
37G	Waldie, Kenneth
24H	Wenckus, John
24A	Williams, Candace
29A	Zarba, Jr., Christopher

11 Crew   **76** Passenger   **5** Hijacker

SEAT | PASSENGER

American Airlines Flight #77

BOEING 757

AmericanAirlines

Row Number 1 2 3 4 5 6 9 10 11 12 13 14 15 16 17 18 19 20 21 22 23 24 25 26 27 28 29 30 31 32 33 34

ZONE A - FIRST
22 SEATS

ZONE B - ECONOMY
154 SEATS

SEAT	PASSENGER	SEAT	PASSENGER	SEAT	PASSENGER	SEAT	PASSENGER	SEAT	PASSENGER
5E	Alhazmi, Nawaf	27C	Debeuneure, James	5A	Hall, Stanley		May, Renee	18C	Simmons, Jr., George
5F	Alhazmi, Salem	27A	Dickens, Rodney	1B	Hanjour, Hani	24F	Menchaca, Dora	20D	Sopper, Mari-Rae
12B	Almihdhar, Khalid	5B	Dillard, Eddie		Heidenberger, Michele	12A	Moged, Majed	4B	Speisman, Robert
17D	Ambrose, Paul	9C	Droz III, Charles A.	21F	Jack, Bryan	6E	Newton, Christopher	19D	Steuerle, Norma Lang
15A	Betru, Yeneh	22F	Edwards, Barbara	2E	Jacoby, Steven	3E	Olson, Barbara	20F	Taylor, Hilda
1E	Booth, Mary Jane	23A	Falkenberg, Charles	26F	Judge, Ann C.	13A	Ornedo, Ruben	24C	Taylor, Leonard
20E	Brown II, Bernard	23C	Falkenberg, Dana	18F	Keller, Chandler	14C	Penninger, Robert	12F	Teague, Sandra
	Burlingame III, Charles	23B	Falkenberg, Zoe	21C	Kennedy, Yvonne	2B	Ploger III, Robert	23D	Whittington, Leslie
4E	Calley, Suzanne M.	26D	Ferguson, James J.	21A	Khan, Norma	2A	Ploger, Zandra	9D	Yamnicky, Sr., John D.
10A	Caswell, William E.	2E	Flagg, Darlene	15D	Kincaid, Karen	13D	Raines, Lisa	21D	Yancey, Vicki
	Charlebois, David	22D	Flagg, Wilson	13F	Lee, Dong	13C	Reuben, Todd	23E	Yang, Shuyin
25D	Clark, Sarah	3B	Gabriel, Richard		Lewis, Jennifer	22C	Sammartino, John P.	23F	Zheng, Yuguang
25E	Cottom, Asia	6F	Gray, Ian		Lewis, Kenneth	18A	Simmons, Diane		

SEAT PASSENGER

6 Crew   53 Passenger   5 Hijacker

![UNITED AIRLINES]

United Airlines Flight #93
BOEING 757

SEAT	PASSENGER

ZONE A - FIRST
24 SEATS

ZONE B - ECONOMY
158 SEATS

SEAT	PASSENGER	SEAT	PASSENGER	SEAT	PASSENGER
17D	Adams, Christian		Bradshaw, Sandra W.	20C	Garcia, Andrew	17C	Marcin, Hildagard
3D	Alghamdi, Saeed	4B	Burnett, Jr., Thomas	11A	Glick, Jeremy	10F	Martinez, Waleska
6B	Alhaznawi, Ahmed	15D	Cashman, William	11D	Grandcolas, Lauren	10A	Miller, Nicole
3C	Alnami, Ahmed	12D	Corrigan, Georgine		Green, Wanda	12F	Nacke, Jr., Louis
	Bay, Lorraine	19C	Cushing, Patricia	16D	Greene, Donald	14A	Peterson, Donald
10D	Beamer, Todd		Dahl, Jason	2A	Gronlund, Linda	14C	Peterson, Jean
17F	Beaven, Alan	2B	DeLuca, Joseph	19A	Guadagno, Richard	5B	Rothenberg, Mark
4D	Bingham, Mark	15C	Driscoll, Patrick		Homer, Jr., LeRoy W.	17A	Snyder, Christine
20F	Bodley, Deora	2D	Felt, Edward	1B	Jarrah, Ziad	18F	Talignani, John
12B	Britton, Marion	19B	Folger, Jane	18A	Kuge, Toshiya	11F	Wainio, Honor
12C	Britton, (extra)	13A	Fraser, Colleen		Lyles, CeeCee		Welsh, Deborah
						21C	White, Olga Kristin

7 Crew **33** Passenger **4** Hijacker

United Airlines Flight #175

BOEING 767-200

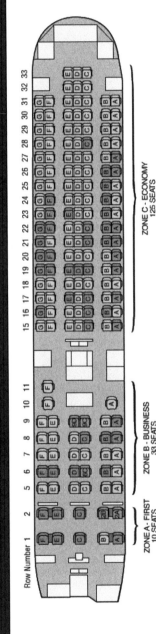

Row Number 1 2 5 6 7 8 9 10 11 15 16 17 18 19 20 21 22 23 24 25 26 27 28 29 30 31 32 33

ZONE A - FIRST
10 SEATS

ZONE B - BUSINESS
33 SEATS

ZONE C - ECONOMY
125 SEATS

SEAT	PASSENGER
2A	Ahmed, Fayez
9D	Alghamdi, Ahmed
9C	Alghamdi, Hamzi
6C	Alshehhi, Marwan
2B	Alshehri, Mohand
22G	Avraham, Alona
6F	Bailey, Garnet "Ace"
19F	Bavis, Mark
6B	Berkeley, Graham
15C	Bolourchi, Touri
21A	Bothe, Klaus
8A	Brandhorst, Daniel
8B	Brandhorst, David

SEAT	PASSENGER
6E	Cahill, John
20A	Carstanjen, Christoffer
21G	Corcoran III, John
17C	de Araujo, Dorothy
9A	DeBarrera, Ana Gloria
	Fangman, Robert J.
22A	Frost, Lisa
8C	Gamboa, Ronald
23F	Goodchild, Lynn
23B	Goodrich, Peter
22B	Gowell, Douglas
1C	Grogan, Francis
16C	Hammond, Jr., Carl

SEAT	PASSENGER
19C	Hanson, Christine
19E	Hanson, Peter
19D	Hanson, Sue Kim
24F	Hardacre, Gerald
24B	Hartono, Eric
2C	Hayden, James
17E	Homer, Herbert
	Horrocks, Michael
16B	Jalbert, Robert
	Jarret, Amy
22C	Kershaw, Ralph
21B	Kimmig, Heinrich
	King, Amy

SEAT	PASSENGER
19A	Kinney, Brian
	LaBorie, Kathryn L.
16G	LeBlanc, Robert
19G	Lopez, Jr., Madovio
1E	MacFarlane, Marianne
	Marchand, Alfred G.
20G	Mariani, Louis
26A	McCourt, Juliana
26B	McCourt, Ruth
28C	Medwig, Deborah
21C	Menzel, Wolfgang
23E	Nassaney, Shawn
20F	Pappalardo, Marie

SEAT	PASSENGER
1A	Quigley IV, Patrick
25B	Rimmele III, Frederick
22F	Roux, James
1F	Sanchez, Jesus
	Saracini, Victor J.
2E	Shearer, Mary Kathleen
2F	Shearer, Robert
6D	Simpkin, Jane
15A	Sweeney, Brian
	Tarrou, Michael C.
	Titus, Alicia N.
17A	Ward, Timothy
27A	Weems, William

9 Crew   **51** Passenger   **5** Hijacker

To comrades, friends, victims, and all of the loved ones whose lives were forever changed on September 11th, 2001.

- J.R. Reiling

Requests for permission to make copies of any part of the work should be submitted online at info@mascotbooks.com or mailed to Mascot Books, 560 Herndon Parkway #120, Herndon, VA 20170.

Library of Congress Control Number: 2014912047
ISBN-13: 9781620867242
CPSIA Code: PRB0714A

Printed in the United States

www.mascotbooks.com

ORDINARY DAY
A Novel of 9/11

BY J.R. REILING

9/11 Chronology of Actual Events

0746: American Airlines Flight 11 pushes back from Boston's Logan International Airport terminal (scheduled start 0745)

0758: United Airlines Flight 175 pushes back from Boston's Logan International Airport terminal

0759: American Airlines Flight 11 departs Boston's Logan International Airport for Los Angeles

0801: United Airlines Flight 93 pushes back from Newark International Airport terminal (scheduled start 0800)

0809: American Airlines Flight 77 pushes back from DC Dulles International Airport terminal

0814: United Airlines Flight 175 departs Boston's Logan International Airport for Los Angeles (scheduled departure 0800)

0814: American Airlines Flight 11 hijacked

0820: American Airlines Flight 77 departs DC Dulles International Airport for Los Angeles (scheduled departure 0810)

0842: United Airlines Flight 93 departs Newark International Airport for San Francisco

0842-0846: United Airlines Flight 175 hijacked

0846: American Airlines Flight 11 crashes into One World Trade Center

0853: Two F-15 fighters take off from Otis Air Force Base, Massachusetts

0851-0854: American Airlines Flight 77 hijacked

0903: United Airlines Flight 175 crashes into Two World Trade Center

0928: United Airlines Flight 93 hijacked

0937: American Airlines Flight 77 crashes into the Pentagon

0942: FAA orders all aircraft in the continental U.S. to land

1003: United Airlines Flight 93 crashes near Shanksville, Pennsylvania

1025: President Bush authorizes shoot-down of hijacked aircraft

CHAPTER ONE

0600 – Harrisburg, Pennsylvania

Elliott Graham woke up in an empty bed.

He smiled to himself, enjoying the afterglow of his favorite dream of the family trip to Vermont where he had taught Tiffany and the kids skiing. Tiffany must already be up and getting the kids ready for school. Elliott shifted easily, not remembering Tiffany taking the heavy coverlet off the bed, but always grateful when she did. He must be coming out of a deep sleep, because he was still disoriented by the odd angle of light curling around the edges of the window shade. Elliott swung his legs out of the bed and confusion abruptly gave way to pain.

"Shit!" he grabbed his knee. "Why the hell did Tiffany move the nightstand next to the bed?" The adrenaline rush seemingly made the walls close in. Then he realized they were closer. Everything in the room was wrong, but familiar…suddenly he forgot the pain as it snapped into place.

"How did I get back in my old apartment?"

0602

Elliott arose and let muscle memory guide him to the light switch on the wall. The resulting illumination only added to his confusion. He *was* in his Pennsylvania Place apartment in Harrisburg right on 301 Chestnut Street. But he wasn't just back in it; he was in it the way it used to be. Exactly. The furniture, the lava lamp Tiffany had "accidently" broken after they moved in together, everything was the same.

"If this is a dream, why does my knee hurt? And why do I need to pee?" He limped into the bathroom and passed the familiar dirty blue shower curtain. After relieving himself, he turned on the faucet to splash water on his face, remembering that hot was to the right on this one. The shock of the cold water was matched by his instinctive flinch as his hands sensed the bristles along his jawline.

When did I regrow my beard? he wondered absurdly as he flicked on the light and was startled at the bizarre apparition looking back at him.

"I'm young."

0604

The hair was jet-black. The crows-feet were gone. The surgical scar on his shoulder was gone, as was the ever-present dull pain. Even the love-handles. He looked to be in his mid-twenties, at least ten years younger than the man who had gone to sleep the previous night.

"What the hell? When did I get back in such good shape?" He didn't mind that part, but it did set his mind racing once again.

But what day? Hell, what year? And how did I get here? Why did I get here? Am I dreaming? Is this a practical joke? Am I in danger? He had had a couple of glasses of wine with dinner the previous evening, and he felt pretty relaxed when he went to bed, but that should not have made him so drunk that he was imagining all of this. Dream or not, he felt hungry, and was willing to go through the motions until he could figure out what the hell was happening. Looking over, he saw his old Pitt sweatshirt hanging on the towel rack (another habit Tiffany had broken him of), put it on, and strolled out to the kitchenette, hoping against hope that something other than bachelor food would be molding in the refrigerator. On his way through the living room he turned on the television to see if he could get some help figuring out which day it was; hopefully it wasn't a workday.

0608

No luck. Apparently his morning feast would be variations of stale bread, candy bars, water, and soda. He smiled as he remembered his standard old joke: Why did they even bother putting vegetable drawers into refrigerators for single guys? "I miss you already Tiffany." Elliott didn't feel like cleaning a dish or glass from the pile sitting in the sink.

0611

Elliott walked back into the living room chewing on a candy bar and clutching a soft drink. He flipped over from ESPN to ABC and saw a vaguely familiar face.

Elliott swept the books and papers out of his easy chair, eased himself into its familiar folds, and took a long drink from the soda can and began languidly flipping through channels until he found *The Today Show* going to commercial. The screenshot came in with the familiar logo and the day's date at the bottom.

September 11th, 2001

0615 – Colgan Air Flight 5930

Mohammed Atta sat in his seat in row 9 (the last row in the plane) on Colgan Air Flight 5930 en route from Portland, Maine, to Logan International Airport, Boston. He had been selected for extra screening at Portland, but that had been anticipated. None of the team members carried anything illegal that could put their great mission in jeopardy. The Americans made it so easy, telling you everything they would be looking for. What had not been anticipated was that since they were changing airlines in Boston, they would need to check in a second time when they got there. When he bought the ticket he had been assured that he would have "one step check-in." Now, he understood that that only applied to the U.S. Airways portion of the trip. Atta had been upset by this unexpected development and was close to getting into an argument with the agent at the counter, but instead complied with that man's recommendation that they hurry if they were going to make their flight. It would not be fatal to their plan, and they had more important things to do that day than argue with infidels. He had gotten his black shoulder bag through security (his travel partner Abdulaziz al-Omari carried a similar bag). Now settled in for the short flight, he resisted the urge to glance over at al-Omari. Everything was going according to plan today, a day that would truly strike fear of Allah into the unbelievers.

0616 – Harrisburg, Pennsylvania

Elliott continued to stare blankly at the television without seeing the commercials.

Is it possible? How is this possible? Why is it happening to me? Is there a reason why it is happening? The thoughts tumbled together in his mind. Elliott enjoyed science fiction as much as the next person, but he was able to regain his disbelief rather quickly once he left the theater. *But this? What could have happened?*

Maybe it was still a dream, but the discomforts of banging his knee and his morning hunger pangs (not to mention enjoying the candy bar) made that seem unlikely. Plus, the apartment was so exact that he was remembering details he had long forgotten, like the three stained, mismatched Oktoberfest coasters on the U-Move-It packing box next to the couch. Maybe he had gone through some sort of time travel to end up back here? But if he did that (and he didn't remember getting placed in a time machine, willingly or not), shouldn't he have come back as a thirty-seven-year-old man, not a twenty-four-year-old? Too bad, that would have implied that someone had sent him back in time, giving his presence in this of all days a purpose instead of simply being an incredible coincidence.

A purpose…could 9/11 be changed?

Could he change it? Certainly if there was a day he remembered that needed to be changed it was 9/11. Thinking back on that day still brought him chills; remembering the carnage, the smoke, the jumpers. So many innocent lives had been lost, and mostly what Elliott remembered was a vivid feeling of helplessness as the attacks had unfolded, not knowing who had started them or when they would stop, and not being able to do anything about it. He dreaded the thought of having to live through the day again, reliving all the pain and the feeling of utter isolation. But now he was apparently not helpless. Some fate had possibly decided to give him an opportunity to change the terrible memories. He was here, and to paraphrase Descartes, "I eat Snicker's, therefore I am." If he were in fact here, maybe he could change things. Maybe he could make a difference. Elliott leaped out of the chair and ran back into the bedroom, looked around and found his old watch lying in the usual spot on the dresser (next to the condom 3-pack). He looked at the time as he slipped the watch onto his wrist.

0622

Did he have enough time? When did the attacks happen? It was early: well before noon. He remembered that on the day of the attacks he had just finished his first class of the day and walked into the teacher's lounge to see the first tower already burning. That would have been about nine in the morning. So he had…two hours, maybe two and a half, to try and remake the past. What to do? He couldn't possibly drive to the place where the attacks had originated from in time to stop them, or to the places where they would end. They were too far away. Another option was to simply call the police. Better still, he could call security at the airport. But which airport? Elliott was pretty sure the hijacked planes had originated out of Boston. Wasn't the airport in Boston named Logan? He needed to get onto a computer. He hurried back into the living room and his big desktop computer monitor on the dining table. Elliott pushed the button and waited for the computer to power up.

What would he tell them, assuming he could even communicate with the people here? He tried to recall the details of the attack. Four planes were taken over, five hijackers on each one, armed with knives and box cutters. Didn't they have bombs, or maybe fake bombs? The attackers had planned it for years and had spent a great deal of time and money learning how to fly passenger airliners, but they had not learned how to land. *Arab men, Saudis*, he thought. They were all members of the terrorist group al-Qaeda, a group that had already been known in America before this day, though they had not yet attacked here. They rode on the targeted flights prior to the attacks, and regularly traveled to and from Europe. Damn, this computer seemed a lot slower than it had the first time he owned it!

0626

Finally Elliott saw his home page come up on the screen. He put in Lycos. When it came up he typed "Boston" and "airport" and "TSA" and hit enter. There was an entry for Logan International Airport; but nothing referencing the TSA. He clicked on the first link. The airport home page came up. *What lame graphics computers had in 2001. At least we had the Internet.* He clicked on "Contact Us." Still no entries for TSA, where was it? Then he remembered that the Transportation Security Agency had been created as a direct result of 9/11: no TSA would be available today. He saw that there was a general number for the airport. He found a paper and pen in a drawer and wrote the number down, then found his old flip cell phone *(old for 2014 of course; I actually just bought it about two months earlier)* and called the number.

"Good morning, Logan International Airport."

"Would you please connect me to the security office?"

"One moment, please."

The operator had acknowledged him, some good news. At least Elliott now knew he wasn't an ethereal presence passing unseen and unheard.

"This is Vasily, may I help you?"

Elliott suddenly wished he had practiced this conversation before he picked up the phone. "Uh, yes are you head of security at Logan?"

"I am the deputy security officer here. How may I help you, sir?"

"Look, I know everything there is probably quiet right now, but it won't stay that way."

"And why is that, sir?" Vasily could feel his annoyance rising. *Prank callers.*

"You are going to have a terrorist incident there. Well, not there actually, but they are going to start there."

"What kind of terrorist incident?" *I don't have time for this.*

"A hijacking. No, several hijackings. Maybe as many as four."

"Four hijackers?"

"No, no, four planes, five hijackers per plane." Elliott remembered the twentieth hijacker. "Except for the one plane that only has four."

"Which plane is that?"

"I'm sorry, I don't remember."

"So there may be as many as twenty hijackers getting ready to seize as many as four different planes at our airport, but you don't know the planes?" *Usually the prank calls come late at night.*

"Yes. But they might not all be working at your airport. But if there are other airports, they are all on the East Coast." *I think?*

"Do you know the airlines?"

"Ah, I think some of the planes are United."

"How do you know this?"

"It's not important." Elliott was finally able to focus his mind. "The hijackers are Arabs, mostly Saudis. They will use box cutters to take over the planes. Some of them know how to fly. Their planes will be taking off within a couple of hours."

"What are their names?"

"The only one I remember is the ringleader, Muhammad A-something. Atak or Attar or Atta, a short name."

"How do you know all this?"

"I just do."

"Sir, I recommend you go repeat your story to your local police department." *Make him someone else's problem.*

"You don't have that kind of time."

"What is your name and where are you from?" That usually ended these conversations.

"Elliott Graham, from Harrisburg."

"If you remember anything else, go talk to your local police department Mr. Elliott Graham."

Elliott sensed where this conversation was going. "You don't believe me."

"I'm skeptical."

"These aren't ordinary hijackers. They're suicides. They are going to take those planes and crash them into the World Trade Center and the Pentagon."

"Goodbye, Elliott."

Graham heard the line go dead.

0634 – New York, New York

Billy "Scoop" Esposito was preparing to leave for work. He was a partner at the Cantor-Fitzgerald trading firm, a capital markets investment bank whose most lucrative asset was its license to trade in U.S. government securities directly with the Federal Reserve Bank of New York. Billy was known as Scoop by his coworkers for his uncanny ability to be the first to know about important business matters. He was a generous man who lived his motto "if you have it, give it." He would buy Broadway tickets for family and friends and always cooked a massive dinner every Christmas Eve for up to sixty guests. He enjoyed being with his family and tried to be a part of their lives as much as possible.

His office was located on the 104th floor of the firm's corporate headquarters at One World Trade Center.

0635 – Logan International Airport,
Boston, Massachusetts

What a nut, Vasily thought. *How many times did this guy say he couldn't remember? As if you could have trouble remembering the bomb plot you know all about. And the past tense lapses were pretty amusing too.* However, putting "Arab" and "terrorist" in the same sentence did activate a latent cultural vibe in the second-generation Ukrainian. While growing up, he had heard family stories of battling Muslims that went back generations into the past. At any rate, standard operating procedures meant Vasily needed to at least check it out. This sounded like a good job for one of the new data-crunchers. When it turned out to be nothing, then he would have to waste more time notifying local authorities to go arrest the guy. What a crummy start to the day. He picked up the phone and dialed the security staff room.

"Are Mohana or Will in yet?"

Vasily was further annoyed by the answer from the other end of the line.

"Okay, whichever one gets in first, have them pick up the recording for the conversation I just finished and analyze it for validity."

0636 – Harrisburg, Pennsylvania

Elliott replaced the phone on the receiver. He probably shouldn't have been too surprised at that outcome.

Should he try again? That guy didn't sound very interested. Assuming they recorded the conversation, there really weren't any other details that he could add beyond what he had given them. Another call to Logan would probably get him arrested. There was no point in trying to contact other airports since he didn't know which ones to call. How about the FBI? He was a little nervous about having agents breaking down his door after a call to the national law enforcement agency. Instead, maybe he could start attacking this problem from the other end. He walked back to his computer and searched "New York Police Department." Getting the number, he walked back to the phone and began dialing. He dialed seven numbers before abruptly slamming down the phone.

Alright how do I get this phone call right? Elliott thought. It wasn't going to do any good to come off sounding like an idiot. Stick to the facts, try to control the conversation, keep it short. He got up and strolled about the room while he thought through his key points, found that the combination of physical and mental exercise helped calm him down, and finally sat back down and dialed the full number.

0641

"NYPD switchboard, may I help you?"

Elliott responded, "Yes, ma'am, I want to report a terrorist threat."

"Go ahead, sir."

"Within the next three hours, nineteen Arab men, mostly Saudis, will use box cutters to hijack four different planes from Logan International Airport and possibly other East Coast airports. Some of them are pilots and they will fly the airplanes into both towers of the World Trade Center."

"How do you know this, sir?"

"I just do. Please evacuate both of the World Trade Center towers immediately. Goodbye."

That was a little better, Elliott thought.

0642 – New York, New York

Ann checked the trace output for the call flagged by the operator. The number was from Harrisburg, Pennsylvania. That made it a federal matter. She immediately dialed the extension for the FBI liaison office to the NYPD.

0643

Police Officer Moira Smith, New York Police Department 13th Precinct, shield number 10467, was saying goodbye to her husband and two-year-old daughter and preparing to go to work. The 13th Precinct was located in the lower portion of Midtown Manhattan, and included Gramercy Park, ConEd, and a number of insurance company headquarters.

Moira was born in Brooklyn and had joined the NYPD in 1988. Her most memorable. day as a police officer had occurred in 1991, when she responded to a subway crash in Union Square that killed or injured over 130 people. She earned the Police Department's Distinguished Duty Medal that day for her efforts that helped save dozens of lives. She enjoyed adventure even on vacation, running with the Pamplona bulls while travelling in Spain.

Today she did not anticipate to be much out of the ordinary, but you never knew, and that is why you came prepared.

0644 – Harrisburg, Pennsylvania

Elliott began typing in "Pentagon" on the computer to get a contact number for that building. When it came up, he wrote it down on the piece of paper and walked back to the phone. He began dialing when suddenly he felt a cold rush as he realized that another phone call from the same number, combined with his Internet searches, was placing him in danger of being tracked by the authorities. He didn't mind getting caught at some point, but he did want to postpone it as long as possible so that he could alert as many different agencies as possible. After he was apprehended, the police were probably not going to be amenable to terrorist threat calls being made from their jail cell. He needed to call from another phone to be safe. He decided to leave his apartment and go down the block to the nearby 7-Eleven and make the call from there. He secured the cell phone to his belt, put on his shoes, and grabbed a ball cap and his keys as he left the apartment. He didn't need a jacket; he still remembered what wonderful weather this day had had.

Detective Bill Smith had arrived at the Harrisburg, Pennsylvania Police Bureau branch located on 123 Walnut Street promptly at 0630 per his normal daily routine. His family had owned a farm in Amish country where he grew up, but when he graduated from high school, he promptly moved to the capital city and joined the police force. He had been promoted from patrolman three years earlier, and was already Deputy Day Shift Supervisor. He missed the action of being out on the street, and most of the officers he was close with were the flatfoots, but he had found that he liked being an investigator and applying his mind to solving crimes. Harrisburg wasn't a big city, but it was big enough to bring a steady supply of mysteries to his desk. He enjoyed the area and couldn't see himself wanting to leave Harrisburg to go anywhere else or move into a different career. He was sifting through his morning email traffic when he received a call from the FBI liaison to the Harrisburg PD that a bomb threat had been made to NYPD from a phone number in Harrisburg, registered to a Elliott Graham, requesting police be dispatched to the address immediately. He passed the number and address to the desk sergeant who would make the dispatch call. Then Smith returned to his computer and began to search the police database for all records related to Elliott Graham. The activity that came back on Mr. Graham, apparently a college professor at Dickinson College in nearby Carlisle, was sparse: two parking tickets and a citation for jaywalking were all that he found on the odd caller sending bomb threats to a city in another state.

0650

Elliott realized that he had forgotten his wallet just as he was approaching the pharmacy on Market Street. He had planned on using a pay phone to make his next call. Now he had to go all the way back to his apartment. He turned around and headed back at a slightly brisker pace. As he walked along, he continued to see familiar faces and places; the traffic officer, old graffiti on the buildings, the florist, the same street potholes. Even the smells on the street seemed to bring back memories of the past to Elliott. Part of him wanted to linger and take it all in, but he needed to keep moving until he had gotten the word out, at the very least. Perhaps he would have time to look around later, although he had no idea when that might be or how he would know his self-appointed task was done. He turned the corner back to Chestnut Street but was brought up short by the sight of the police car parked directly in front of Pennsylvania Place apartments. He instinctively knew why they were there and tried to appear nonchalant as he quickly reversed his path without being noticed by the officer standing outside the vehicle.

0653

Patrolman Williams called the Harrisburg PD dispatch office and notified them that no one had responded when Patrolman Heraclius knocked on the door of apartment 407. He then requested a physical description of Elliott Graham which they could use to ask around and determine if anyone had seen the suspect recently.

0654

Graham knew that the police had already traced his calls back to his apartment. He continued walking while he was thinking. The police would probably get a physical description of him as well. Now what was he supposed to do? He couldn't go back to his apartment. How could he make phone calls without any money? Since he did bring his keys, he could have gone to his car and rooted around in there to try and find some change under the seat or in the ashtray, but his car was in the building's off-street parking, so he doubted that he could get to it without the police outside his apartment seeing him, especially since by now they would probably have his license number as well. Now he had no money, no safe area, and police already starting to beat the bushes for him. What to do? Whatever he did, he needed to keep moving away from his apartment. His heart was racing, but he tried to keep from walking so fast that he attracted attention to himself.

0655 – Logan International Airport, Boston, Massachusetts

Marwan al-Shehhi had kept the call from the pay phone brief, using their prearranged code to tell Mohammad Atta that Marwan's hijacking team was in position to board United Airlines Flight 175 which was scheduled to depart at 0758 from Logan to Los Angeles International Airport. He now knew that Atta's team was also ready; from this point on, both of the teams of mujahedeen would be on their own.

0656 – Harrisburg, Pennsylvania

Patrolman Williams had obtained Graham's physical

description from the station and told Heraclius to wait by the squad car. They had also located Elliott Graham's car, so Heraclius would be responsible for watching both while Williams would begin to canvass the neighborhood looking for anyone who might have recently seen the suspect, whom the station said was a white male in his mid-twenties, five foot seven, black hair and eyes, 170 pounds.

0657

"Good morning, sir!"

Elliott swung around, surprised by the first person of the day to recognize him. It was the guy who ran the corner kiosk he sometimes got a paper from.

"Hi." *The guy is staring right at you. Say something, Elliott!* "How are you?"

"Are you all right, sir? You look a little confused."

Elliott had an idea. "I am, but I just locked myself out of my apartment. Do you have a telephone I could borrow to call my girlfriend? She has a key."

Ed Moeller smiled. This guy wasn't a big customer, but he was a steady one. "Certainly, sir." He handed over his cell phone.

Elliott took it and pulled out the note with the Pentagon number.

"You gave a girl a key to your apartment, but you don't know her number?"

Ugh. Think fast. "Yeah, she just changed the number."

At that moment another customer (the pretty girl from the Laundromat, one of Elliott's favorites) brought Ed's attention to the other side of the kiosk. Elliott was glad for the distraction. Hopefully she would prevent the kiosk owner from noticing him dialing more than seven numbers as he was making his call.

After a couple of rings, "Pentagon switchboard, how may I direct your call?"

"Security, please."

"I'm sorry, do you mean national security or the Pentagon complex?"

Huh? "Your security there."

"One moment, please." Elliott glanced over at the kiosk owner who was still focused on his attractive customer.

"This is Mister James with installation security, how may I help you?"

"I need to report a terrorist threat to your building."

"What sort of threat, sir?"

"Arab men, terrorists, are going to hijack planes and fly them into several buildings including the Pentagon."

"Military planes or civilian?"

"What?"

"Are they hijacking civilian planes or military?"

"What? They're hijacking civilian airliners that they are riding on, you know, as passengers."

"How are they going to crash these planes into buildings?"

"They're suicides, they know how to fly. They will take over the planes and crash them into the buildings." Elliott glanced over as the Laundromat girl walked by him and gave him a nice smile.

"You need to evacuate the Pentagon immediately." Elliott snapped the phone shut and handed it back to the kiosk owner, who was eying him curiously. "Thanks man, I appreciate it. She's on her way." Then as a final thought, "Sometimes it's a pain getting that girl to go out of her way."

Ed smiled at that. "Hope your day gets better, sir." He thought the guy seemed a bit agitated, even for someone who was locked out of his apartment. Now he's walking in the opposite direction from the one he came in, and as Ed looked close he could see the guy had a cell phone strapped to his belt. *What the hell? Why did he want my phone if he already has one? I hope the guy didn't call Japan on my phone.* Further thought about the odd incident was cut off by the retired postal worker in his gray fedora stepping up for his daily coffee with sugar.

0658 – Washington, DC

Max Beilke was preparing for his scheduled morning meeting at the Pentagon. Max was a retired Army master sergeant from Minnesota who had been drafted into the Army in 1952, serving for two years in Korea. He decided he liked the Army and made it into a career, meeting his wife while stationed in Germany and eventually earning his bachelor's and master's degrees attending night school. Max's career culminated when he was sent to Vietnam in 1972 while the negotiation for withdrawal of U.S. forces was underway. He was officially listed as the last American combat soldier to leave Saigon on March 29, 1973, boarding a C-130 transport aircraft for home on live TV.

Today's meeting was part of his post-service career of helping provide services for Army veterans and their families. As Deputy Chief of the Army's Retirement Services Division, he had helped improve medical and benefit plans for retirees and even authored an online newsletter called *Max Facts* that addressed retiree concerns.

One more small reason to enjoy coming to work was that the one-fifth section (it seemed like they did everything in the Pentagon by fives) or "wedge" where he worked had just had renovations completed on it. The Pentagon looked impressive from the outside, but in reality, it was a hastily-constructed World War Two building that needed all the help it could get. He also looked forward to getting back home to catch up on his other passion, the Minnesota Vikings. Although they had lost their opening game two days earlier, this weekend they would be just up the road in Baltimore. There were plenty of Ravens fans in the Pentagon. Maybe he could score a ticket from someone in the building and go see the game.

0659 – Logan International Airport, Boston, Massachusetts

Mohana Ushashi of Boston's Logan Airport Security had logged in to her computer to find a request from her supervisor to run a validity check on a potential terrorist threat call received at 0626 that morning. She searched the database to pull up the call so she could listen to it and provide analysis. And all before she even got her first cup of coffee!

0700 – Harrisburg, Pennsylvania

The traffic policeman nodded at Patrolman Williams that he recognized Elliott Graham's picture, and told him he thought he had just seen the guy heading south as he pointed down 2nd Street. Williams radioed back to Patrolman Heraclius, told him to stay in place in case the suspect came back around, and told Heraclius to report back to the station with the details of the situation and that he was pursuing a potential sighting of the suspect on foot.

0701

Another one. Damn! Detective Smith had just taken a second phone call from the FBI LNO on a terrorist threat call from his town. This one was to the Pentagon, from a cell phone registered to an Edward Moeller. However, the address was in a different part of town than Elliott Graham's. But this was a cell phone, so it could be anywhere. Would we really have two different terrorist-related prank callers at the same time? Unlikely. Say it's just one guy, and let's say it's this Graham. So let's assume Graham knows we'll be tracking his calls. So he knows that he needs to call from other phones in the area, so he leaves his apartment and goes...

"Mike, get me a job or work address for an Edward Moeller, fast."

0702

Elliott Graham really didn't know what else to do at this point. Perhaps he should go somewhere else and try to make another call, perhaps to the FBI. He could just turn himself in at the local police station. Perhaps he could go check to see if his apartment was clear.

0703

Patrolman Williams took the call, listened and scanned the street in front of him. "Okay. I do see a kiosk about half a block in front of me. I'm on my way."

0704

Ed Moeller saw the policeman hurrying toward him.

"Sir, did a guy just use your phone?"

"Yes, Officer, it couldn't have been five minutes ago. He used my cell phone even though I think he had one of his own and then took off that way. He looked pretty agitated."

"Do you know him?"

"He is a regular customer of mine, but I don't know his name. I think he lives-"

Patrolman Williams cut him off. "We know. May I please see your phone, sir?" Ed handed it over. Patrolman Williams punched "redial" and listened. As soon as he heard the word "Pentagon" spoken on the other end, he was on his radio calling in an on-foot pursuit, providing the physical description and requesting backup.

0705 – Logan International Airport, Boston, Massachusetts

Mohana first decided to run a check to see if she could get a match on the purported Arab name the caller had identified, and brought up the data base for registered passengers for outbound Logan flights from now until noon.

0706 – Harrisburg, Pennsylvania

Elliott heard the sirens coming at him from down the street and knew he was out of options. Flight would probably not further his cause. He could even get shot, which he didn't particularly want, and it certainly wasn't going to help stop the terrorists. He calmly stepped onto South River Street and slowly waived with both hands outstretched at the approaching squad car.

0707

Detective Smith took the call from the desk sergeant notifying him that Elliott Graham had been apprehended by the officers in the arriving vehicle responding to Patrolman Williams' request for backup. He had promptly identified himself to the officers and had not resisted arrest. The officers would be bringing him back to the station shortly. Detective Smith asked the desk sergeant to notify him upon their arrival and expedite Graham's initial processing.

0709 – Logan International Airport, Boston, Massachusetts

Mohana had found a match. The passenger database showed that there was a reservation on American Airlines Flight 11, scheduled to depart Logan at 0745 for LAX, for a Mohammed Atta. Even though the caller had specified United Airlines, she sensed this was the right flight to continue researching. She pulled up the full reservation list for Flight 11 and started looking carefully for men with Arabic-sounding names.

0710 – Harrisburg, Pennsylvania

"How much longer to the station?"

"A couple of minutes, sir," Patrolman Evans responded. Evans didn't think this guy seemed like much of a threat. He had seen enough wild-eyed crank call suspects to know that Mr. Graham didn't fit the profile. Well-groomed, quiet, didn't appear to be drunk or on drugs. So why in the world had he started making threat calls? "Why, are you in a hurry?"

"Believe it or not, I am, Officer."

Evans didn't believe it.

0711 – Logan International Airport, Boston, Massachusetts

Mohana was up to at least eight names on Flight 11. She was not an expert on Arabic names, but her best guess was:

Atta, Peter el-Hachem, Waleed Iskandar, Abdulaziz al-Omari, Rahma Salie, Wail al-Shehri, Waleed al-Shehri, and Satem al-Suqami. Two of them, el-Hachem and Salie, were U.S. citizens. Salie was also female, although the caller hadn't specified that they had to be male. Another name, Iskandar, was from England. That left five names of Egyptians and Saudis, including the name specified by the caller. That sounded like something she needed to report in. She picked up the phone and dialed Mr. Vasily Rostov.

0712

Vasily sat forward in his chair. "Have you checked any other flights?"

"No, sir," Mohana responded.

"Okay, good work. Continue searching and call me back if you get anything else. How many more flights might there be again?"

"There might be up to three more according to the caller, sir."

"Okay, thanks."

0713

Irene O'Donnell, supervisor of security at Logan's Terminal B, picked up the phone "This is Irene."

"Irene, it's Vasily. We had an anonymous tip of Arab hijackers grabbing a plane out of Logan. Your American Airlines Flight 11 had a potential match including number of hijackers, nationality and even the name of one of the suspects. Get a team over there as soon as you can."

"Yes, sir."

Vasily knew they were still a long ways from a terrorist

situation. The tip could have been phoned in by someone who hacked into the flight manifest, or just someone who knew these guys were on the plane and had a personal grudge against them. But best to be sure and have security go check the situation. That's what they got paid to do.

0714 – Harrisburg, Pennsylvania

Patrolman Evans pulled up to Harrisburg PD and brought Elliott Graham inside. The desk sergeant must want this one to move through fast; she had already printed out the initial custody papers and begun filling them out. Maybe this will turn out to be an important arrest. Evans smugly thought of how that would piss Williams off even more than he had been when he came huffing and puffing (*lazy toad, maybe you should lay off the doughnuts once in a while Buddy!*) up to Evans just as Evans had been putting the suspect into his squad car.

As the desk sergeant completed the paperwork she told Evans, "Please take the suspect to Room Two and wait for Detective Smith."

"Yes, ma'am."

0717 – Logan International Airport, Boston, Massachusetts

Mohammed Atta was trying to keep his annoyance from boiling over. Years of planning and they had not caught that the transit from Colgan Air Flight 5930 to American Airlines Flight 11 at Logan was going to require another checkpoint screening for himself and Abdulaziz. They probably should have all just stayed in Boston the night before, even though they had discussed that option and ruled it out because of the possibility that that many Arab men checking into the airport at once might arouse suspicion among the airport security personnel.

Atta had been born in Egypt in 1968, although he sometimes told people he was from the United Arab Emirates. He was the third child and only son of middle-class, educated parents. His father in particular had been a stern, reclusive figure who did not allow Mohammed to play with the other children in the neighborhood. Mohammed consequently excelled in his studies, and graduated from the elite architecture program of the University of Cairo in 1990. He worked for the Muslim Brotherhood-affiliated Engineer's syndicate until his father convinced him to continue his graduate studies in Germany in 1992.

Mohammad then spent a number of years moving between jobs in Germany. In the process, he ostracized his roommates, partly due to his aloofness and partly due to his odor; he rarely bathed. After he began attending the Al-Quds Mosque in Hamburg, he found their fundamentalist and militant version of Islam to be to his liking. In 1999, he had decided to travel to Chechnya to fight the Russians, but changed his mind at the last minute and went to Afghanistan instead. There, he met the leader of Al-Qaeda, Osama bin-Laden, a legend among radical Muslims around the world. Bin-Laden was looking for English-speaking Mujahadeen and convinced Atta to participate in what the quasi-fugitive terrorist was calling the "planes operation."

Atta threw himself into the project, attending flight training, scouting potential airports from which to hijack planes, and assisting in getting other team members into the United States. He had become so busy that his driver's license had been revoked *in absentia* when he failed to appear in court for a previous citation. He didn't care; he wouldn't need a driver's license where he was going.

Despite the minor problems, the good news had been that Marwan had called to notify him that his team was in place and prepared to begin the operation. Hopefully, the brothers at the other airports were moving ahead with the operation as well. He now saw that they should have had better communications set up to verify that all operations would proceed as planned, but too late to worry about that now. Everything still looked to be going according to their plan; Allah wills all.

0718 – Harrisburg, Pennsylvania

Detective Smith had watched from his office as they brought the suspect into the interrogation room. He was quietly obeying all instructions from the officers attending to him, not at all like the usual wild-eyed threat suspects one would expect to see. He walked into the holding room and took the table seat opposite from the suspect. "Good morning Mr. Graham, I'm Detective Smith. Can I get you some coffee?"

"Yes, please."

"Any preference?"

"Just some cream or milk, please."

Definitely polite, seems a lot like an academician. "Patrolman Evans, would you be kind enough to get Mr. Graham a coffee?"

"Yes, sir." Evans departed slowly, understanding the routine but annoyed that the detective had not asked him for any additional information or even acknowledged his effort in capturing Graham. How soon they forget after they make detective...

"Do you smoke?"

"No." An odd question that Graham had not heard in some time. He had a small flash of appreciation for the cultural shift America had experienced during the last thirteen years, because no one in 2014 would offer a cigarette to someone in a public facility.

"I assume the officer read you your rights?"

"Yes, sir."

"Would you like us to get you a lawyer?"

"No, sir."

"Okay. You understand you can change your mind at any time and request counsel?"

"Yes, sir."

"Very well then. You've been very busy this morning, haven't you?"

"Yes, sir."

"It looks as if you have already made at least two threatening phone calls, to the NYPD and the Pentagon."

"No, I wasn't threatening them, I was warning them of a terrorist threat." For the moment, Elliott decided to hold off telling him that the number was actually three.

So much for having to coerce him. "So what is the threat?"

"Nineteen men, Arabs, mostly Saudis, are going to hijack four airliners from Boston and possibly other airports in the Northeast. Their leader is a guy named Mohammed Atta or Akka, I'm pretty sure. They will use knives and box cutters to take over the planes. After they take control of the planes, they will fly them into the World Trade Center, the Pentagon and another place in Washington."

"Where in Washington?"

"I don't know."

"Why don't you know if you know the other destinations?"

"I just don't know the last one."

"Why the odd number of hijackers?"

"One guy isn't going to show up."

"Why not, will he chicken out?"

"I think he wasn't able to get into the United States."

"Why not?"

"I think he had visa problems, or he was on the FBI's watch list."

"What's his name?"

"I don't know."

"Do you know the names of any of the other guys?"

"No."

That line of questioning was turning into a dead end. "What time will all this happen?"

"What time is it?"

Interesting question. Smith glanced at the wall clock. "It is 7:25 in the morning."

"The planes are probably going to start crashing before 9 this morning, so they will probably be taking off within an hour."

"Who is setting their schedule?"

"What? Well, no one, exactly. They are from al-Qaeda."

Smith thought for a moment until the connection hit him. "The group that blew up our embassies in Africa?"

"Yep."

"Okay." This guy certainly didn't fit the usual prank call profile. "So what is it that you do for a living, Mr. Graham?"

"I am a professor at Dickinson College."

"You look a little young to be a professor."

"Assistant professor. Of English."

"So how does an assistant professor of English at Dickinson

come to know about terrorist plots against New York and the Pentagon?"

"I wish I had an answer that made sense."

"What answer do you have?"

"Can I hold off on answering that for a while?"

"You can do whatever you want sir, but I can't properly evaluate the validity of your information unless I know your source. You don't really look like an Arab terrorist, or someone that hangs around with them."

Elliott knew the tipping point was upon him. "Okay, here goes. When I went to bed last night it was March 24, 2014. When I woke up this morning I was here."

Let the games begin. "So…you're from the future."

Smith's response had come so condescendingly that it was obvious he was not seriously considering Elliott's answer. Why should he? And what else could Elliott say? "Yep."

Patrolman Evans' return with coffee broke the ensuing uncomfortable silence in the room.

0726 – Logan International Airport, Boston, Massachusetts

Mohammed Atta prepared to board American Airlines Flight 11. Looking around the departure area, he saw that the remainder of the team had joined him and Abdulaziz: Waleed al-Shehri, his brother Wail, and Satem al-Suqami all appeared calm and ready to carry out the will of Allah. The others had stayed in Boston the night before and driven a rental car to Logan in the morning. All three of the Boston-based members of the team had been selected by the Computer Assisted Passenger Pre-screening System (or CAPPS for short) as passengers requiring additional prescreening. Waleed had checked no bags, so only Wail and Satem had been selected for the additional scrutiny of having their bags screened for explosives. They had anticipated this of course, so none of them were carrying explosives or illegal weapons. Atta was confident that their plan, specifically designed to defeat the known American security procedures, would get them onto the airplanes with the tools they needed to succeed. In Sha Allah.

0727 – Harrisburg, Pennsylvania

Patrolman Evans' interruption gave Detective Smith the opportunity to collect his thoughts. He had certainly seen his share of nuts, but this was the first one to claim being from the future, as opposed to just being able to predict the future *Okay, there was that one girl, but she was on something non-prescription and flying higher than a kite at the time.* For such a far-out story, the guy certainly didn't appear to be much of a physical threat. He appeared well-groomed and calm, concerned but not anxious, certainly not a flight risk.

"So tell me more about how you got here. Who sent you?"

Elliott knew that a long stretch of uselessness was coming, and all he could do at this point was wait it out and not lose his temper, which wasn't going to help anyone, certainly not the people he was trying to save. "I don't think anyone sent me."

"You came on your own?"

"It isn't a mission or a trip. I don't know why I'm here."

"So is this who you are in the future?"

"No, this is what I was like in 2001, thirteen years younger. I mean, what I looked like. I mean, what I look like to you. I have all my 2014 knowledge and memories."

"And this is where you lived back then, which is now?"

"Yes, same apartment, same stuff in it, people I haven't seen in ten years going about their normal routines outside."

"Are any of the attacks going to happen in Harrisburg?" *Better ask, just in case.*

"No."

"Then why did you come back here?"

"I didn't come and I wasn't sent, at least as far as I know. I told you, I just woke up this morning in my old room."

"And you decided to go running out the door and spend your day trying to stop these attacks?"

"Yes."

"That is very noble of you, why do it?"

"They're that terrible. Nearly 3000 Americans will die today from these attacks. What else am I going to do, go teach first-year English?"

"Isn't that too many people for four airplanes?"

"It isn't just the passengers. The World Trade Center Towers in New York will end up collapsing, killing the people trapped inside.'"

"I'm sorry, the whole building is going to collapse?"

"Both of them."

"Have you called anyone besides the NYPD and Pentagon?"

Oh boy. "Yes, I contacted Logan International Airport." Now he had gotten Smith's interest. "I have made a total of three calls this morning. However, they weren't much more interested than you are at this point."

Not exactly a lie, but a deliberate omission, so Smith knew that the suspect was aware that the police were not going to be happy to find out that there had been more calls. "Sir, I will ask you again if you want a lawyer, because if your story does not bear out, you could be liable for making false threats. Do you want a lawyer?"

"No."

"Very well. As long as you are fully aware of your rights, we'll continue. Do you remember who you talked to at Logan?"

"He said his name was Vasily."

Smith wanted to verify all the calls this guy had made; the more he had, the easier it would be to make the charges stick in court. Smith turned away from Elliott. "Patrolman Evans, could you please contact security at Logan Airport in Boston for me and ask for Vasily?"

"Yes, sir." Patrolman Evans moved toward the main area.

"And please leave the door open on your way out."

"Yes, sir."

Smith turned back to Graham. "Did you contact anyone else?"

"No."

"Why did you leave your apartment?"

"I suspected my phone was being traced and I wanted to make as many warning calls as I could before I got rolled up."

"So you knew you would end up getting arrested?"

"Probably, yes. I'm not stupid. I'm just trying to do the right thing. I assume that what I did could be considered illegal."

"We'll see. So why make anonymous calls? Why didn't you just come into the station and report it?"

You're kidding me, right? "Because I figured you wouldn't believe me."

Good point. "Do you know any of these hijackers personally?"

"No."

"Have you ever been in the military or police?"

"No."

"Any sort of armed organization or paramilitary group?"

"I was in the Cub Scouts for a couple of years when I was a kid."

Smith was fairly confident he could rule out extremist organization membership but if not, it would eventually show up on the background checks here and at the FBI. "So what is your interest in reporting this? You were correct in guessing that you were going to end up in the police station. Why does an assistant professor in Harrisburg, Pennsylvania want to get himself in trouble over something that will happen in New York and Washington?"

"I told you, because 3000 people are going to be killed. It is a national catastrophe that will scar our entire country for years and generate two wars in the Middle East. I'm not much of a civic duty nut, but this is something a person simply has to try and stop. It's just the right thing to do."

"Are you married?"

"Not yet. Is that an important question? I told you this thing is going to happen pretty soon."

"All my questions are important to me. I sympathize with your anxiety, but I have no evidence regarding this future disaster other than your predictions. Right now New York and DC aren't going to listen to me any more than they are to you. Even if I were inclined to believe you, and to be honest, at the moment I'm not. What do you want me to do?"

Elliott was silent at that. The detective was right. Certainly they would begin to believe him after the first plane was hijacked, but he couldn't stomach the thought that he couldn't change fate now. *Do we really have to wait until a plane crashes?* "Well, perhaps you could…"

The phone on the desk rang at the same time Patrolman

Evans yelled, "Logan Airport in Boston for you, Detective. It's hot."

0732 – Logan International Airport, Boston, Massachusetts

Mohammad Atta took his seat 8D on American Airlines Flight 11, trying to watch casually as the rest of the team filed onto the plane and took their seats. Still no sign of alertness on the part of the passengers or crew.

0733

Marwan al-Shehhi was happy that the infidels still seemed blissfully unaware of the presence of his team of warriors in their midst. He, Fayez Banihammad, Mohand al-Shehri, Ahmad al-Ghambi and Hamza al-Ghamdi were trying to avoid eye contact or conversation as the attendant began her pre-boarding announcements as United Airlines Flight 175 prepared to back out of Terminal C for its scheduled flight to Los Angeles.

0734 – Dulles International Airport, Washington, District of Columbia

Hani Hanjar hated being in Washington DC, even though he was the only team leader who had lived in the United States before the "planes operation" had even been conceived by the al-Qaeda leadership. He was also the only team member who had wanted to fly planes as a career before becoming part of al-Qaeda, with his applications being rejected multiple times by Saudi Arabian Airlines. At this point, he could only hope that there would be no major problems before American Airlines Flight 77 could get in the air, after which they could fulfill the will of Allah.

0735 – Newark International Airport, Newark, New Jersey

Ziad Jarrah was anxious as he worked his way through Newark Airport toward the departure lounge for United Airlines Flight 93. He had been arguing with the al-Qaeda planners almost since the inception of the operation, and had even threatened to withdraw from the mission at one point. Alone among the operation members, he was still close to his Lebanese family and girlfriend, and had even visited her in Germany less than two months earlier. This upset Atta, the overall leader of the operation, despite their closeness dating back to their Hamburg days. Al-Qaeda seriously considered replacing Jarrah with another mujahedeen, but in the end he was allowed to remain. Allah seemed determined to test his faith right through to the end. He was going to be the only team leader operating with less than five members. The normally comatose Americans had denied Mohamed al-Khatani entry into the country the previous month; the organization made a mistake in sending him to the U.S. on a one-way airline ticket with insufficient funds to demonstrate that he could support himself. Al-Qaeda had failed to produce a replacement in the short time remaining, leaving him, Ahmad al-Haznawi, Ahmed al-Nami and Saeed al-Ghamdi with the daunting task of subduing an entire crew and passengers and piloting the aircraft to its target. He would have preferred to have all the teams leave from the same airport, but it was too difficult to find four long-distance flights with proximate takeoffs leaving from the same airport. With one of the later scheduled takeoff times, Jarrah knew he had the greatest likelihood of having to fight a hostile group of infidels who were aware that many aircraft seizures were occurring, and might already know that the other aircraft were being used as flying bombs. Perhaps it was appropriate that the most difficult team leader would have to execute the most difficult mission. "Allah will provide."

0739 – Logan International Airport, Boston, Massachusetts

They were almost there, Mohammed Atta knew. The flight attendants were closing up the overhead bins and preparing the cabin for departure. Pushback from Terminal B was scheduled for 0745, and everything looked like it was proceeding right on schedule. Atta planned to make one last phone call to al-Shehhi and his United Airlines Flight 175 team on his cell phone as they got onto the runway. He wanted to make sure that at least their two teams would be attempting to carry out their attacks that day, because everyone understood that once one happened, the Americans would change their security.

0740 – Harrisburg, Pennsylvania

"This is Detective Smith."

"Good morning, Detective, this is Vasily Rostov, Deputy Chief of Logan International Airport Security. I understand you have a suspect in custody who is claiming there will be a terrorist attack today using hijacked aircraft."

"Correct."

"We had someone call about an hour ago claiming he knew of a terrorist plot originating out of our airport."

"That sounds similar to what my suspect is telling me."

"Well, the thing is, we got a match on the name he gave us, Mohammed Atta."

Elliott saw Detective Smith glance at him for the first time that morning with an expression other than bemused condescension.

"Have you checked out this Atta guy?"

"My security is on the way. What is the guy telling you?"

"That there are several teams of Arabs that are going to try to hijack commercial planes in the U.S. and use them as flying bombs to crash into buildings like the World Trade Center towers and the Pentagon. He says they are real hard cases, fanatics."

"All of which may or may not be true. Still, is the suspect available?"

"He's sitting right here. Do you want to talk to him?"

"Hell yes!"

Detective Smith hit the speaker button on his phone as he looked at Elliott with a mixture of amusement and curiosity. "It's for you."

0743 – Logan International Airport, Boston, Massachusetts

Karen Martin, lead flight attendant on American Airlines Flight 11, was mentally preparing for her preflight orientation briefing to the passengers when she was startled by banging on the aircraft door.

0744

Mohammed Atta also heard the banging and watched with dismay as three out-of-breath Americans wearing suits came onto the plane. He could see the bulges under their jackets as well. They all looked at a piece of paper held by the eldest member who whispered something to the lead flight attendant, then the three men split up and began moving further onto the plane. One stopped next to Waleed and Wail. Another moved slowly past him as the older black man following behind stopped right in front of him. *Please, not now!*

"Mr. Atta, I'm Mosi Rossiter, Logan security. Would you please get your personal items and come with me?"

0745

Vasily's intercom line was ringing. He instinctively glanced at the phone ID even though he knew who it would be. Mohana. "Mr. Graham, stay on the line." With a growing sense of urgency he pushed a button on the phone. "Yeah."

"Sir, I found another one. Five more Arab men are manifested for United Flight 175 out of C19."

Another LAX flight. "Get Robin and have her draft an FAA warning based on the threat message." In his excitement he punched out the phone call to Harrisburg as he was attempting to start his own intercom call. Finally he redialed. "Will, call the pilot for UA 175 and don't let him push back from the gate. Get a team over there now to check out five passengers. The names will be waiting for your people when they get to the gate."

0746 – Harrisburg, Pennsylvania

"Detective, I think it was just cut off." Graham finished his statement as he realized that the phone had been on speaker, so Smith already knew too.

"Well, we'll wait for a callback. How do you know these people?"

"I don't know them. I told you, I'm from the future."

"Yeah, but that was before a shred of your story actually checked out. Now quit bullshitting me and tell me how you knew these people would be on the plane!" Smith used obscenities on the rarest of occasions. This seemed like a good time for one.

"Dude, I don't understand it either."

"Don't call me 'dude'. Look, I was mentally preparing to charge you with making false threats, but now this is going to start turning into obstruction of justice, which is going to be a whole lot worse for you! You need to start coming clean and telling me what you know."

0747 – Logan International Airport, Boston, Massachusetts

Mohammed Atta was seething inside as he and his team were led to a small room just off from the departure gate. As they entered, the request came from the eldest agent, the black man, for them to empty their pockets and carry-on items and place everything onto the table in the middle of the room. *How had they found out about the team? Who tipped them off?*

0751

Vasily was beginning to feel overwhelmed by the pace of events as he saw a call coming in from security area B1.

"Go ahead."

"Sir, this is Mosi Rossiter. We pulled those guys off the flight and checked them out. All of them were carrying Swiss Army knives, box cutters and a Leatherman, which are all legal items although I have never seen anyone carrying a box cutter before. They claim they are draftsmen and that they use them for work.

One of the guys had a can of mace, which is also legal. One guy also has some little boxes and wires that they could in theory fashion into a made-for-TV-quality fake bomb."

"Are they carrying anything illegal?"

"No, sir."

"How are they acting?"

"A couple of them look really nervous and sweaty. The leader, Atta, is calm although he's acting pretty pissed and arrogant, like he owns the place. He's talking about lodging a complaint with the Egyptian Embassy."

"Hold on." Vasily really wished his boss were here and not laid up at home with a cold. He dialed the airport manager.

0752

Paul Simpson picked up. "Good morning, Jose."

"Sir, it's Vasily. Jose is still sick. We have a problem."

"Go ahead."

"We got an anonymous phone call this morning that groups of Arab men were going to hijack several airplanes here at Logan to fly into buildings in the U.S. He provided a name that we matched with a passenger on American Flight 11, an Egyptian named Mohammed Atta. We pulled him and four other Arabs off the plane and they were all carrying knives and even box cutters, just like the caller said. One of them was also carrying a can of mace. It's an unusual bunch of stuff, but it is all permissible. United Airlines Flight 175 also has five Arabs on board: I am holding the plane and I have a team going to Terminal C now to check them out as well."

"Have any of them done anything illegal yet?"

"No, sir."

"What do you recommend we do?"

"Sir, I don't think we should let them fly."

Paul did not like that idea at all. The airports already had to deal with a steady stream of complaints from Middle Eastern countries that their citizens were subject to discrimination when traveling in the U.S. *Gee, you think?* Paul thought to himself. But of course he couldn't say that officially. "What did the FBI say about these guys?"

"They haven't raised an alarm yet, sir."

What was he supposed to do? Pulling Arabs based on an anonymous tip was just going to create hell for him. "How did the caller know about them?"

"He didn't say, sir."

Paul's other phone began to ring. He glanced at the caller ID: American Airlines. *Oh boy, here it comes.* "American is on my other phone, wait." "Good morning, this is Paul."

"Why are you holding Flight 11?"

"There is a security problem we are trying to resolve Joel."

"Well Christ, you guys are costing us a shitload of money while you play your paranoid games. How much longer are you going to dick us around?"

As if I wanted to have this conversation. "We got a tip that several Arab passengers on the plane are going to hijack it with box cutters."

"Box cutters? Are you shitting me? What are they going to do, paper cut the passengers to death?"

"Two of them actually had box cutters, the others had knives. They also have Mace."

"None of that stuff is illegal, right?"

"Well no, but doesn't it seem a bit suspicious to you?"

"If we kept every suspicious passenger from flying with us we'd go broke in about a month. Unless you're going to reimburse their tickets."

Thanks for the economics lesson. "Are you willing to let these guys on your plane?"

"Take the knives and box cutters, put 'em in a bag in the cockpit, they can have their stuff back when they get to LAX."

"Are you sure?"

"Yeah, let's get going, all right?"

"What about the Mace?"

"Confiscate it."

This isn't elementary school. "It's their personal property."

"Christ, I'll personally give them a frigging gift certificate when then get to LA!"

Color me surprised. "Okay then. For the record, I don't think this is a good idea, but it's your airplane." Back to the intercom. "Vasily, let them on the planes on condition they give up the box cutters for the pilots to hold until they get to LAX. Leave the Mace behind."

Vasily figured that his boss had spoken to the airline and was expecting a response about like this. "Sir, I don't think that's a good idea. These aren't random guys. Two of them are brothers, they're carrying odd weapons, and they're all up in first class where they can get to the cockpit pretty fast. This isn't a random bunch of guys."

"Vasily I hear you, and I just told American the same thing, but right now they haven't done anything illegal and American is willing to let them travel—"

Vasily cut in, "Sir, you know as well as I do that the damned airlines would let The Jackal fly as long as his check clears."

"Vasily, I still hear you, but they aren't on a threat list. If we hassle these guys we're just going to end up with another complaint. This isn't Russia, Vasily."

Rostov felt his temper shoot up at that one. "I know damned well where we are. And my family is Ukrainian, sir."

Paul knew he was dangerously close to crossing a line. "Sorry, my friend, I was just trying to make a point. Let them go."

"Both flights, sir?"

"Yes."

"Yes, sir."

0755

Mohammed Atta now knew they had made two major planning mistakes, the first in assigning team members. It had seemed smart to put brothers such as Waleed and Wail al-Shehri on the same teams, because they would work effectively together when the time for action came. Their other problem was that the planners had become fixated on edged weapons, particularly the box cutters, as the weapon of choice, even though most people in America don't routinely carry them. Now, with five foreigners including two brothers carrying the same unusual weapons pulled from the plane and placed in the same room, it was obvious even to the complacent infidels that they were working together. The can of Mace had made their precarious situation even worse. Atta had to make a decision, and he didn't like either choice. The infidel had informed him that he and his team would not be allowed to re-board the plane carrying their weapons. The weapons would be carried by the crew and returned to them in LA. They would also have to give up the can of Mace. Atta could choose not to have his team board their aircraft and abort the mission. However, he had gotten the call from Marwan al-Shehhi that his team was in position and ready to board United Flight 175.

At this point, the Americans were not going to allow him to make an unmonitored call, so all he could go on was the last information he had, that Marwan's team was going ahead with the mission. He didn't know how the mission had been compromised, so he didn't know if any of the other teams had also been betrayed. If Marwan's team, or any other, completed the mission, the Americans would doubtless tighten up their security in the future. He and the others had understood during planning that even the beneficent Allah would only provide them a single opportunity to strike this blow at the infidels. The Americans had been trained not to resist during hijackings, so he felt he still had a good chance to seize control of the aircraft. Perhaps they could still succeed; if not, the confusion created by an attempted attack might help the other teams. He knew that the other members of his team would follow his lead. In Sha Allah.

"You can expect that I will file a complaint against this airport with the Egyptian consulate the moment I land in LA."

Mosi wasn't happy with the situation either, but he had his orders. He was also getting annoyed at the guy's insinuation that they shared some kind of secret bond just because of Mosi's skin color. *Buddy, I have nothing in common with you.* "I understand, sir. Please accept our apologies. The safety of our planes and passengers are always our primary concern. You are all free to re-board at this time."

0756

Marwan al-Shehhi wished that he could talk to Mohammed Atta again. An hour ago, their plan seemed to be on its way to success. Now, United Flight 175 seemed a thousand miles away from he and his mujahedeen. If he called Atta, he might find out what their current status was, but there was no way he could do so without giving away Atta and the coordination of their teams. The American security official had told him that he would confiscate their weapons and Mace and they would have to travel to LAX without them. Marwan was considered a friendly person, not a common trait among the team members, and he was the youngest of the team leaders, so he was trying to use his charm rather than bullying his way onboard, which he suspected was not going to work. Marwan was also trying to feign ignorance of the other team members, but the Americans did not seem to be buying his subterfuge. Perhaps they had already gotten to Atta; that would explain their heightened sense of security towards his team. If they had, then he could also expect greater attention to be paid to them and the flight itself. If Atta's team did succeed in their mission before he and his team were well into theirs, it seemed highly unlikely that they would be allowed to fly into the objective without some attempt at a shoot-down. A prime condition for success had been the assumption of surprise creating a slow U.S. response. Without it, it seemed unlikely that they would be given the time to complete their Jihad. They had put in so much time and preparation that would go to waste if he tried to push what was turning into a bad position by pitting an unequipped team against a heightened infidel response system. Apparently, Allah had willed another destiny for him and his team. Up to this point they had done nothing illegal, so they would be able to depart the airport without interference. Clearly His will was to be obeyed, In Sha Allah.

"This is an outrage! I will not allow myself to be insulted in this manner. These men may do as they wish, but I will not. I am leaving this place of shame immediately and you will be hearing from our embassy today!" They had agreed during planning that this would be the standard threat teams would levy against prying infidel officials in the unlikely event that the integrity of the mission was being placed in jeopardy.

The American security official was nonplussed. "As you wish, sir. Have a nice day."

Marwan al-Shehhi tried to keep his temper under control as he headed for the airport exit. Since one of Atta's team members, Satam al-Suqami, had stayed with them at the Milner Hotel in Boston the night before, it seemed like a logical place to reassemble his team. If Marwan did not hear from Atta or the other teams soon, he and his team probably needed to start heading north.

Fayez Banihammad followed his leader Marwan al-Shehhi with great regret, even though his instincts told him that a day like today would never come again. He was fully prepared to be martyred for Allah, but did not see how they could successfully accomplish their mission without Marwan. None of the others knew how to fly, so at best they would only be able to glide the aircraft into the nearest available town or building. The World Trade Center had been specifically chosen by al-Qaeda, as had all the other targets. If New York was the financial capital of America, then the towers were its unique symbol. Striking at them (as previous mujahedeen had done in 1995 with partial success under the divine guidance of Sheikh Omar Abdel-Rahman) was striking at the greed and corruption of capitalism and its evil cousin, democracy. The plane and its passengers were only a tool with which to strike a blow that would resonate throughout the Dar al-Harb (all places on earth that were not members of the community of believers following the teaching and practice of the Prophet, Peace Be Upon Him).

Without a famous target at the end, their carefully planned mission would be just another suicide truck bombing, albeit one inside the United States. Fayez felt, as Marwan also undoubtedly did, that Allah had a greater purpose for their team, and so was willing to wait patiently for His will to reveal itself. As their Pashtun brothers in Afghanistan were fond of saying, "I waited a hundred years to take my revenge. My only regret was that I acted in haste."

The al-Ghamdi brothers exchanged glances at each other and the other team members as they were departing the holding area. They had not lost their enthusiasm for the mission, and were not about to turn tail and run. Instead of turning right along with Marwan al-Shehhi to the airport exit, they walked left and began confidently moving toward the departure gate.

Mohand al-Shehri glanced to the right at Marwan and Fayez slinking out of the airport, then to the left to see the self-assured step of the al-Ghamdi brothers. He quickly made his decision and also turned to the left. Three mujahedeen were still a powerful force!

Marwan al-Shehhi sensed that not all of the team were following him out of the airport, but dared not glance back while still under the gaze of the infidels and could only try to hide his anger and frustration as he continued to stride along his chosen path.

0757

Phillip LeBarge, the security official responsible for Terminal C, watched the three suspicious passengers walking toward the plane as well as the departing ones, all of whom were trying too hard not to look at each other. He still didn't like this situation and picked up the phone to call the Gate C19 ticket counter.

"Steward, is there an air marshal on United Flight 175?"

"No, sir, none that I am aware of."

Phillip thought about that. "Okay, I'm getting one now. Three of the five people we pulled off the plane are choosing to board. I'll be down there in a few minutes."

"Yes, sir."

0758

Daniel Lewin was not happy to see his fellow passengers return to Flight 11.

He was an Internet entrepreneur, having co-founded Akamai Technologies, but previously, he had served as an officer in the elite Sayeret Matkal of the Israeli Defense Forces. Known simply as "The Unit" in the IDF, they were trained and experienced in a wide variety of reconnaissance, counter-terrorism, and hostage rescue missions. If there was one thing Daniel felt sure he could spot, it was Arab males up to no good, and these guys fit that bill in spades. Whatever bullshit act they had played on the airport security, the way the Arabs (they looked like peninsula Arabs, probably Saudi, Wahhabi fanatics with his luck) avoided looking at each other made it obvious to him that they were working together. Hell, the two all the way up front could be brothers. With four in front of him and one behind, Daniel realized that, if things went bad, he was going to have to be ready to move fast. He knew Americans tended not to resist hijackers and he might not get a lot of help from his fellow passengers, but he also knew that Arab hijackers had a nasty habit of killing Jews they found during their attacks, and he wasn't going down without a fight, even if he did it alone.

Daniel turned to the pleasant-looking gentleman sitting next to him. "Sir, I have some loose threads on my shirt. Do you happen to have a knife or something like that with you that I could use to remove them?"

0759 – Dulles International Airport, Washington, District of Columbia

Gilbert Monceaux heard the notification bell for the FAA alert message system located near his desk at Dulles International Airport. He walked over to the printer and took the message from the feeder tray and read:

Logan International Airport responded to an anonymous tip regarding a potential hijacking and found a group of five Arab men armed with box cutters on a flight bound for LAX. Tipster also said that East Coast airports are potential departure locations for other armed groups of 4-5 men departing in the morning.

Monceaux promptly went back to his desk and called his assistant researcher and told him to run the tip against their passenger lists and get back to him right away if he found any matches.

0800 – Logan International Airport, Boston, Massachusetts

Phillip Le Barge walked up to the counter at gate C19 as the three Arab men were handing their tickets to the plainly distraught steward.

"Sir, I will assist you with seating these passengers. What seats are they scheduled to be in?"

Robert Fangman had never been so happy to see airport security and tried to be polite and professional. "Mr. al-Shehri is in seat 2B. Mr. al-Ghamdi is in seat 6B and Mr….oh, you're Mr. al-Ghamdi too. You are in seat 6A."

Right near the cockpit, eh fellows? No way that that was going to happen, Phillip thought to himself. "Follow me please, gentlemen."

0800:30 – Dulles International Airport, Washington, District of Columbia

Hani Hanjar was seated on American Airlines Flight 77, along with the remaining members of his team, Salam al-Hazmi, Nawaf al-Hazmi, Majad Maqed and Khalid al-Mihdher, spaced behind him in the aircraft. The al-Hazmi brothers had been selected for extra screening, but eventually they had all been able to board the aircraft without incident. All of their planning and preparation seemed to paying off for them. Ten minutes until scheduled departure and everything was going according to the plan and Allah's will.

0801 – Newark International Airport, Newark, New Jersey

Ziad al-Jarrah sat in seat 1B wondering why they had not left at the scheduled time. The rest of his short-handed team was nearby, with Ahmed al-Nami and Saeed al-Ghamdi in row 3, and Ahmed al-Haznawi back in row 6. Al-Haznawi had his bag undergo additional screening for explosives, but none of the others had encountered problems. US aircraft frequently departed late and they had not expected all the planes to be on time; that was why the early teams were expected to wait after takeoff before beginning their operations. Nothing to worry about yet.

0801:30 – Logan International Airport, Boston, Massachusetts

Phillip LeBarge led the three men to the back of the half-full aircraft, grateful to see that there was only one other person in the last half dozen rows of the aircraft. He pointed out the three empty seats 30G, 31F, and 31G, and wrote the numbers down on a slip of paper.

"Sit there, please."

Hamza al-Ghamdi angrily responded, "This is not my assigned seat. I have paid for first-class ticket. Why am I being placed here?"

"Actually you paid for business class, but you are sitting here because I am placing you here. In fact, I want you to sit in 30G. Your brother can sit in row 31. If you don't like it, you can deplane the aircraft. But if you want to go to LAX, this is the seat you will sit in to get there."

Mohand al-Shehri glared at the brothers as he said to the American security agent, "So be it. You can expect I will demand a refund of my money for the seat that I paid for when we arrive in California, as well as filing a complaint with my embassy."

Phillip saw that the two brothers had lapsed back into silence. At this point, surly compliance still counted as compliance. "Very well. Have a safe flight gentlemen." He strode to the edge of the airplane, making note of the civilian passenger configuration along the way, without losing sight of the troublemakers until he saw his friend Jeremy Blivens quickly approaching from around the corner of the departure tunnel, with the familiar firearm bulge in his jacket. Phillip stepped off the plane and handed him the slip of paper.

"I called for an air marshal because this is a potential problem on this plane. That's why you got tagged. There are three of them Jeremy; here are the seats I relocated them to from first class. Five were pulled from the plane originally, two chose not to re-board. They were carrying knives and Mace but we confiscated all of that. They have been showing a lot of attitude, but they haven't been violent yet. They are all young Arab males. I bunched them up so you can keep an eye on them: there are plenty of empty seats for you around the early 20s."

Jeremy thought they were making this harder than it needed to be. "Why don't you just not board them, Phil?"

"They haven't done anything illegal and they aren't on any lists we've run. I requested putting a marshal on board as an additional precaution."

"Okay, but this is an unusual procedure. Part of the point of an air marshal is to be hidden. They will probably figure out who I am and I lose the advantage of surprise. I can deplane them on my authority too, you know." Then somewhat wryly as he glanced up at the ceiling, "At least I think I can. I've never even heard of a situation like this."

"I know, Jeremy." Phillip knew that he was asking a lot of his friend, and also knew he was right about being able to deplane the suspects. Phillip would back his friend whatever he decided, but it would get messy down here if the suspects were removed from the plane.

After a long pause, Jeremy said, "What the hell, let's go. If I'm lucky, the Dodgers are playing at home tonight."

Phillip breathed a small sigh of relief. "Thanks Jeremy. Godspeed."

0802 – Harrisburg, Pennsylvania

Detective Smith had grilled Graham pretty hard, but was coming to the conclusion that, whatever his issues, he wasn't a nut. Graham stayed calm and composed, was consistent with his answers, and certainly seemed earnest. The background checks were coming in, and it just wasn't adding up. The guy had never left the United States. Hell, he barely left Harrisburg. No arrest record, membership in radical organizations, history of anti-social writing, didn't own a gun. No financial problems, marital strife, drug use, mental problems, nothing. Not even any relatives with problems. This guy was as average as average could get.

SO how in the hell could he have known that five Arab men armed with box cutters would try to board a plane in Boston that morning?

Smith knew that Logan had issued an FAA warning based on Graham's story and the positive hit they had found at their airport. He was waiting to hear back on more details from Logan or the FBI. The whole situation didn't make sense unless Graham was lying about not knowing the suspects, which Smith didn't really care about as long as his information kept checking out. He was blocking out the whole absurd time travel thing. At this particular moment, there didn't seem to be much else Smith needed to extract from Graham related to the case, but they needed to talk about something.

Smith figured he might as well make this a memorable conversation. "So tell me about the future. Has mankind learned to live in perfect peace and harmony?"

Elliott thought that was slightly condescending, but if he were in Smith's place he would probably do the same thing.

"No."

"Solved world hunger?"

"Uh-uh."

"Cured cancer?"

"Nope."

"Do you guys have ray guns or hover cars or meals in a pill?"

"Give me a break will you? I said I'm from thirteen years in the future, not 200."

Detective Smith masked a laugh to continue his questioning of Elliott. He decided to channel his inner Dr. Emmett Brown.

"Okay, future boy, who's president in 2014?"

"Barack Obama." *What kind of pointless questions were these?*

"Never heard of him."

"You wouldn't have. I think right now he is a state senator in Illinois."

At last, something Smith could check. He moved to the door and yelled, "Jenny, can I jump on your computer for one hot minute?"

"Sure, Detective."

"Sir, let's head out to the main area for a few minutes."

Elliott responded as he started to rise, "No problem."

As they moved outside, Elliott saw most of the officers looking at him with varying degrees of interest. He was uncomfortable with the attention and realized he had preferred the quiet and isolation of the holding room.

Detective Smith logged in and while waiting for his account to come up, he looked at Graham and could clearly see his discomfort. Finally he brought up the Internet and accessed AskJeeves.

He typed in Brock "How do you spell that last name again?"

"O-B-A-M-A."

He typed in the letters and waited.

"Nope, no Brock Obama. Did you say Illinois?"

"Yep."

He added Illinois to the search string and hit return again.

Still no Brock Obama, but there were entries for a Barack Obama, including the Illinois state senator's home page. He hit return. "What kind of name is Barack Obama anyway?"

"I don't know. I think it's African."

The import of that statement sunk in just as the webpage for Barack Obama came up featuring a picture of the state senator.

Elliott noticed the uncomfortably long silence accompanying Smith's bemused stare.

"You are telling me that we are going to elect this guy president of the United States in 2012?"

"Actually, in 2012 we're going to re-elect him."

Smith thought long and hard about that one. Finally he said, "Friend, if you were going to tell me that America is going to elect a black president in 2008, you would have had a better chance of convincing me if you had said it would be Colin Powell."

"I know. Powell never runs."

"Why not?"

Elliott wondered to himself, *Does this guy think I'm the magic answer man or something?* "I don't know. I'm just telling you he doesn't."

"Okay, that's probably all the politics I can stand anyway. Are the Yankees going to win the World Series again this year?" What the heck, maybe if the nut is right, he could make a few bucks out if it.

"I don't follow baseball."

"Basketball?"

"Sorry."

Gimme something here. "Okay, but everyone keeps up with the Super Bowls."

Elliott thought for a minute. "Have the Patriots won any Super Bowls yet?"

Yet? "No." An annoyed no, as their loss two days ago at the hands of the lowly Bengals had cost Smith the opening week office pool, normally the largest of the season.

"A good rule would be to bet on Tom Brady unless he is going up against Eli Manning."

"The backup? Mr. Michigan? Are you kidding me? They just paid Bledsoe about a bazillion dollars to be their franchise quarterback."

"Well, Brady is their guy in the future. I think Bledsoe got hurt." Actually, Elliott thought to himself, wasn't this close to when Bledsoe was injured? Elliott went to the Super Bowl parties his friends threw every year, but just didn't follow the pro game that closely.

"Well, even with Bledsoe, they still stink." Smith replied sourly. "And didn't you mean Peyton Manning?"

"No, his younger brother, Eli."

"I didn't know he had a brother."

"I did say younger brother."

"Peyton Manning has a brother who is even better than he is?"

Elliott did flash a slight look of bemusement. "He is in the fourth quarter of Super Bowls."

Whatever that means. "Well, is Peyton going to win any?"

"Yeah, he'll get at least one."

"Why at least? He's still playing in 2014?"

"And still tearing it up."

Meanwhile AskJeeves had confirmed that Eli Manning was quarterbacking at 1-1 Ole Miss, which didn't sound like a springboard to greatness to Smith. "So do you follow college ball?"

"A little bit."

"Tell me something then."

"Well, if you don't like the SEC now, you're going to hate them in thirteen years. It will get so bad they'll be playing each other in the title game."

"That is bad news to a Big Ten fan like me."

Mention of the Big Ten triggered an impulse in Elliott. "As long as I'm here, I guess I should tell you that someone needs to go investigate Penn State. They have a football coach molesting little kids, the leadership knows but they aren't doing anything about it."

Elliott could tell he had said something wrong again.

"Penn State."

"Yes."

"The one in Pennsylvania? The Nittany Lions? Happy Valley?"

"Yes."

Another long silence.

"Of all the college football programs in America that could be sweeping criminal activity under the rug, the one you pick is Penn State?"

"Yes."

More silence. "You know, every time I even vaguely start thinking about believing you, you come out with a line like that."

"Dude, we are going to be just as shocked in 2011."

"Don't call me 'dude'. I thought you said you were from 2014."

"Yes I am, but this story breaks in 2011. It's going to rock the whole program, and then they'll get sanctioned hard on top of it. It is going to be ugly."

"Fair enough, although that one sounds like a tall tale." *A very tall tale.* "Anything else about the future you think we should know?"

Elliott took another moment to gather his thoughts. "Yeah, okay. Let's see. Saddam doesn't have WMD, Fannie Mae and Freddie Mac are lending money to people who can't pay it back, and the Greeks are cooking their books."

"You might have something with that last one." Smith was about to ask him about global warming when the phone rang.

0810 – Logan International Airport, Boston, Massachusetts

Flight Attendant Karen Martin began her preflight briefing as Pilot Charles Burlingame began backing American Airlines Flight 77 away from the terminal with Hani Hanjar and the rest of his team on board and ready to carry out their mission. Hanjar was getting a bad feeling that things might be going wrong with the other teams and decided that they should start the mission almost as soon as the airplane got airborne. Soon their work could begin, In Sha Allah.

0811 – Newark International Airport, Newark, New Jersey

Janine Parker, Head of Security at Newark International Airport, returned to her desk and found the FAA warning message from Logan sitting in the middle of her day calendar.

She was recovering from an early bout with the flu. She never got the annual vaccine, justifying it in her mind on the grounds that it was usually not available until the middle of winter anyway. Usually she got away with it, but this year her luck had run out. She probably should have been home, but she had used all her sick days and did not want to start burning through vacation time. She read the message, then picked up the phone.

"Lee, please run a check for all our flights, looking for five Arab men flying to LAX."

0812 – Harrisburg, Pennsylvania

Detective Smith and Elliott Graham had just relocated to Smith's office when a call arrived for him. Smith listened briefly, reached over to put the phone on speaker, and then said, "Please repeat that to us again, Vasily."

"We found a second plane that had five Arab men on board with box cutters, knives and Mace. We also put out an FAA warning to the rest of the East Coast. No other planes at Logan fit the profile. How many more planes did you say there are?"

Elliott was grateful that proper authorities finally seemed interested in his story. He hoped it hadn't come too late. "Two."

"What else do you know, Mr. Graham?"

"Nothing. I'm sorry. I've been telling Detective Smith the same thing since you dropped your last call."

"Detective, are you holding Mr. Graham?"

"No, I'm questioning him. I don't have anything to charge him with, particularly since his tips seem to be spot on. He doesn't look like he is in a big hurry to leave the station." Elliott nodded agreement as Smith glanced at him.

"Well don't let him out of your sight. LAX security will probably want to talk to him before these guys land there."

Elliott snapped around in his chair. "You let them on the flights?"

"Yes. They haven't done anything illegal. We confiscated their box cutters and Mace. What else could we do?"

"So after all I've done, there are still two planeloads of terrorists who are getting ready to fly out of Logan?" *Dammit!*

"Some of the guys on the second plane chose not to board."

Elliott's mind was racing. "How many? Is that Atta's team or the other one?"

Vasily was getting a bit miffed at not receiving any sort of thanks for actually acting on this guy's tip. *You're getting pretty bold for a prank caller who happened to be right about something.* "Two of the five did not board on the flight that is not Atta's."

Graham thought intently for a few moments. The second plane team was being broken up. So maybe it was possible for him to change the future. If there were only three guys on the plane, they might not be able to hijack it. But Atta and his team got on their flight anyway. Graham seemed to think that the hijackers had mostly lived and moved along the East Coast. So it wouldn't make sense for them to escape to LA. The second team members who had aborted had probably done the correct thing and left to return to the area they were familiar with. But Atta's whole team boarded. They might not know the status of the other teams, and might not be able to communicate with them once on the airplane.

"Did you let the two groups of men interact with each other?"

Vasily thought, *who is the cop and who is the suspect here?* "No, sir."

So Atta wouldn't know what was happening with the other teams. They had to figure this was a one-shot deal. If any of the teams carried out their mission, none of the others would be able to do it again. If they weren't fleeing, then they had to be...

Elliott was definitive as he said in as calm and clear a voice as he could muster, "They're going to try and hijack your plane anyway."

0814 – Dulles International Airport, Washington, District of Columbia

Hani Hanjar noticed with mounting unease that the plane had turned off the taxiway and was headed back to the terminal. No intercom communication had come from the crew to explain the change, which could only mean that it was due to his team. What could they do? Hanjar had wanted to be a pilot all his life, so unlike the other pilot hijackers he had studied all phases of flying, even if he had not done particularly well in his studies. If they hijacked the plane now, he could in fact take off with this aircraft. But there would be a risk that the airfield authorities could disable the aircraft or block his takeoff. Even if he did take off, it would be an unauthorized departure and would immediately draw a reaction from the Americans, allowing them more time to bring fighter aircraft to intercept the plane and shoot it down before they could reach their target. They had all emphasized over and over that, at this point in the operation, nothing illegal had been done. Better to submit to American snooping than rush through a panicked change of plans for no real gain and possibly jeopardizing the other missions. Perhaps they would be allowed to take off anyway. Stay calm and all would be revealed, In Sha Allah.

0815 – One World Trade Center

As he promptly did every day at this time, Scoop Esposito

called from his office at Cantor-Fitzgerald to check on his wife and two children. He smiled as his daughter told him to "go make money."

0816 – Harrisburg, Pennsylvania

Elliott felt his neck veins starting to bulge out as he continued to talk to the Logan security man. He thought he had been fairly calm up to this point, but now his frustration was beginning to show. "Have you not been listening to me? These guys are fanatics. They're not going to be deterred from their plans just because you took their toys away. Passengers today aren't prepared to stop suicidal terrorists. They don't know what this group of attackers is capable of. They are bad men and they are still going to try and take over that plane."

"What do you mean when you say passengers today? How do you know all this information about these guys?"

"I told Detective Smith already."

"What did you tell him, sir?"

"I don't see how this is relevant."

"I'll decide what's relevant, sir."

Smith broke in. "Vasily, let's you and I chat for a minute. Mr. Graham, would you kindly wait outside with Officer Evans for a minute?"

Elliott saw what Smith was doing and was grateful. Maybe Smith could do a better job of building Elliott's credibility. He certainly couldn't do much worse than Elliott had up until now. He took a deep breath before he responded.

"Certainly, Detective. But I'm telling you that Atta is still a threat, the second flight is still a threat, and there are two other planes out there. This is not close to being over by any stretch of the imagination. Believe me, I wish it were, but it isn't." Any more than that and he knew that he would just start sinking his own standing with Smith.

0817

Smith punched off the speaker function as Graham exited the room. "Hey Vasily, I wanted to send the young man out for just a minute so we could chat."

"Thanks, I'm starting to feel pretty damned unappreciated. What's the deal with this guy?"

"Nothing that matches any line of investigation I have pursued. He is as average as a suspect can get; no priors, no warrants, nothing. There is no logical reason for him to know what he knows. I'm still evaluating him. Don't worry, he isn't going anywhere. Actually, he's been totally cooperative, and doesn't strike me as being a nut in spite of the nutty story he has been telling me. Please keep me posted as you get more information: maybe it will help me shake some more details out of him."

"Do you have FBI there too?"

"Right now I'm trying to just keep it a duet. I don't think it is going to do any good to spook him with a bunch of guys in suits barging in."

Vasily would have to worry about this guy and his story later. "Will do. Sorry for the temper, but I'm kinda having a crappy morning. I have to go. I have a call coming in from Dulles. Let me know if you come up with anything else."

0818 – Dulles International Airport, Washington, District of Columbia

Ann Lemont waited at the departure gate at Dulles for AA Flight 77 to return. In her hand was a list sent to her by her boss Gilbert Monceaux with six names identified by his assistants based on the morning hijacking tip: Hani Hanjar, Salem al-Hazmi, Nawaf al-Hazmi, Majed Moqed, Khalid al-Mihdhar, and Norma Khan.

0819 – Newark International Airport, Newark, New Jersey

Ziad Jarrah squirmed uncomfortably in his seat. Now the delay was approaching twenty minutes. He knew that his team had one of the later scheduled departures, and the other teams would have no way of knowing when all four planes were airborne. During planning, they had considered utilizing the long scheduled flight times to wait as much as an hour before commencing the operation to ensure all planes were airborne, but had rejected that on the grounds that planes deviating from their flight paths for that long would risk shoot-down, even by the indecisive Americans. Plus it would reduce the amount of aviation fuel left in the tanks and thus the size of the explosion. Atta had agreed to wait approximately fifteen minutes after takeoff to begin his team's operation, so they might have already begun. Given the time it should take for the infidels to learn about that hijacking and inform the other airplanes, they were still within a likely success timeframe. Ziad tried to relax and trust in Allah.

0820 – Logan International Airport, Boston, Massachusetts

American Airlines Flight 11 finally lifted off from Logan International Airport thirty-four minutes late carrying a large number of unhappy passengers, none more so than Mohammed Atta. He had anticipated his team being the first one to seize its aircraft, so some delay was acceptable, but his margin for error before other seizures would alert the Americans of their attempt was narrowed, particularly as they would now be starting unarmed against an alerted crew. He thought he could now wait at most ten minutes after takeoff before beginning his operation. Everything had been going so well. How had the Americans been alerted to the presence of his team? It was frustrating, but he tried to relax and trust in the will of Allah.

United Airlines Flight 175 took off at almost the exact same time, carrying several people assessing the situation in order to figure out the best options available to them.

Pilot Captain Victor Saracini and his co-pilot, First Officer Michael Horrocks, had been discussing what they should do since Boston security came over the radio to brief them on the situation. Both were former military members, so they felt they were mentally prepared for any problems that might occur. Knowing that the suspects were crammed in the back of the plane and that an air marshal was on board was a major relief, although both of the pilots wished the men had just been denied boarding in the first place. As the Captain, Victor could probably come up with an excuse to get them off the plane (even reducing their number to two would make him feel a lot better), but he didn't feel like spending the next three months going through inquiry boards and bureaucratic red tape that would keep him from his love of flying. Victor talked to Flight Attendant Robert Fangman and had him collect all spare keys to the cockpit door and give them to Michael. He tried to make his instructions to Fangman as clear and concise as possible.

"We're locking the door behind you. We will not reopen the doors until the plane is on the ground and the engines are off, whatever the circumstances in the cabin might be. If those guys start acting up you let us know and we'll land wherever we are, even if we have to put it down in a farmer's field. Do you understand?"

"Yes, sir," Robert responded and unhappily departed.

Victor turned to his copilot. "Mike, I want you to be prepared to maintain cabin security if we do have to put this thing down fast. If you don't have a knife you can borrow mine."

Mike Horrocks did not think it was a good decision to let the three men on the airplane, but he could see how everyone felt backed into a corner. He was too junior to do much to change the situation other than quit, and he liked his job too much for that, not to mention abandoning his pilot. "Okay, Vic."

Jeremy Blivens was sanguine about his situation, even if it wasn't ideal. He had been en route to serving as air marshal on another flight in Terminal C, so he was a solution ready-to-hand when the call went out for an air marshal on Flight 175. As he walked back through the plane he saw the seats Phillip had recommended, but decided he didn't want any passengers between him and the suspects if they started acting up. He selected 24E, sitting across the aisle from an older gentleman. He tried not to look back at the suspects, but if they were going to be troublemakers, he figured they were already well aware of his presence, so he wasn't going to make a great effort to conceal himself. As he walked past the flight attendants upon entering, he had instructed them not to allow any passengers to relocate to the back of the aircraft as was customary once the outside door had been closed. However, looking at the faces of the passengers, he saw that this had not been necessary. They had seen the Arab men taken off the plane, and some of them returned and put in "time-out" in the back of the airplane, so none of the passengers appeared eager to sit anywhere near them. *This does seem like a damned prison plane*, he thought to himself grimly.

Hamza al-Ghamdi was very unhappy about being separated from his brother. He felt that they should do whatever they could to serve Allah, even without Marwan being there to lead the team. Because Mohand al-Shehri had chosen to board with them, they could still carry out a great mission because his presence on their team had given them an important advantage from the beginning; a spare pilot. Mohand had conducted some flight simulator training in Vero Beach along with Abdulaziz al-Omari and Saeed al-Ghamdi. If they could seize control of the aircraft, Mohand should be able to deliver them into a memorable target. Even if he failed, they could still achieve martyrdom by crashing a plane full of infidels with a spectacular explosion. Hamza had prepared his soul for his great role in the glorious Jihad, and he had no intention of waiting for another day.

Ahmed al-Ghamdi and Mohand al-Shehri were exchanging brief sentences in muted Arabic or using hand signals whenever they felt the stewardess standing in the next aisle was not observing them, although such opportunities were few indeed. Ahmed was fairly sure that the unsmiling man who had gotten on after they re-boarded was an air marshal. He would probably be carrying a pistol, and had placed himself between them and almost all the other passengers, so the only possible hostage was the woman in 28C. They also had no weapons, nor was there any baggage stowed near them to give them a chance to find something to swing or throw, let alone protect themselves from things thrown at them. Unlike the original plan, they had been placed as far from the cockpit as possible, so they would potentially have to fight through the entire compliment of passengers and crew just to get to the cockpit door, which would almost certainly be locked. Ahmed had no problem with becoming a martyr, but he didn't want to do it by getting beaten to death by a bunch of infidels while uselessly lying in the aisle of the airplane. They could choose to do nothing, and assuming none of the other teams launched their missions, they would have to find some place to hole up in Los Angeles until they could return to the East Coast and reunite with the rest of the hijackers. That was easier said than done. None of them were very familiar with the West Coast, he wasn't sure if between them they had brought enough money to get back to Boston (they hadn't needed money for where they thought they were going), and if they were being tailed by the FBI, they had to invent an activity in California important enough to justify first-class airfare across the United States. It would be highly suspicious to have spent thousands of dollars on airfare to go rent a room in a fleabag motel after they got off the airplane. Worst of all, if any of the other teams did act but they did not, they could expect to be detained and interrogated when they landed. They seemed to be in a situation where almost anything that happened was going to end up with them being watched by the police, with little opportunity to carry out their great plan. Mohand was enthusiastic about continuing the mission, and felt confident that he could create a great opportunity for martyrdom for all of them if he could get into the cockpit, but Ahmed was skeptical that there was much of a mission left to carry out. He was beginning to wish that his brother had simply followed Marwan and Fayez out of the airport.

Flight 175 retracted its landing gear and flaps and continued to climb out of Boston's airspace.

0821 – Harrisburg, Pennsylvania

Detective Smith turned back to Elliott. "So are they going to miss you at the college?"

Smith's present tense questioning still seemed odd to Elliott, as if he had asked him if he were going to go to college after he graduated from high school.

"Yeah, I guess so."

"You don't seem too worried about it. What are you supposed to be doing today?"

"Teaching a Literature 101 class."

"Good class?"

"It's okay, I guess. I'm really more of a composition person, but when you're a graduate assistant you take what they hand you."

"That's pretty good memory for over a decade ago."

Graham soured slightly as he responded, "Do you remember where you were when you heard that Kennedy was assassinated?"

Smith had been in fourth grade assembly. "Good point." The guy doesn't get rattled and he hasn't been caught contradicting himself. Smith was glancing through his notes when he suddenly remembered a line Graham had thrown out earlier. "What did you mean when you said you aren't married yet?"

"In 2014, I'm married with two kids."

"What is your wife's name?"

"Tiffany. Her maiden name was Johnston, so actually she's back to being Tiffany Johnston all over again, I guess."

"And your kids?"

"Warren is nine and loves to play baseball. Selina is seven and wants to be a ballerina."

"Nice girl?"

"Of course she is, she's my daughter."

"No, I meant your wife."

That was the easiest question Smith had asked Elliot all morning. "The best."

"When will you meet her?"

"I don't know."

"Why not? I know men are absentminded about things like that, but you don't remember the details about her?"

"I remember everything about her. She lives at 1423 Field Street, Joliet, Illinois. Her parents live at 2038 Oak Street in Dayton. I know her roommate, Heidi Garcon, and I can't stand her in the slightest. They have an old 486 computer, although I guess that isn't too old yet. I know her cat Felix, and how he likes to lick the curtain after you take a shower. I know the furniture in her apartment right down to the ottoman. She drives a blue 1987 Chevy. I know her phone numbers, home and work. Her favorite movie is *The Wizard of Oz*, but she tells people it's *Casablanca*."

A lot of details that Smith could check out. "So how can you not remember when you met her?"

"That's not what you asked me. You asked me when I will meet her. I don't know when I will meet her."

"Why not?"

"Because we met on September 11th, 2001."

0822 – American Airlines Flight 394

Tiffany Johnston was trying to relax, not an easy thing for

her as she did not particularly like flying. She really didn't want to go on this trip, but the hospital was paying for her to attend a medical conference in New York, so she looked at it as a networking opportunity. She loved working as a nurse and enjoyed emergency room the most, but she was also starting to think she wanted to explore life and see what else was out there in the world. Besides, she needed a break from her circle in Chicago. The hospital, her roommate, her ex-boyfriend. Well, maybe not Felix, who was so meticulous about his grooming that he had denuded the hair from his stomach.

Who knows, maybe I'll meet a cute guy this week. She had taken a Dramamine before departure, and tried again to let it send her to sleep.

0823 – Dulles International Airport, Washington, District of Columbia

Ann Lemont had finished questioning Ms. Khan and dismissed her as a potential suspect in less than a minute. She entered the holding room where her two assistants were arguing with the other suspects. On the table were a collection of knives and box cutters.

In a firm voice she said, "Gentlemen, I am Ann Lemont, head of security at Dulles."

She barely got the sentence out before the men turned their attention to her and began screaming and wildly gesticulating.

0824 – American Airlines Flight 11

Mohammed Atta tried to appear casual as he glanced around the cabin at his fellow team members. Everyone was looking back at him except Wail, but Waleed was no doubt relaying to him. Good thinking by Waleed; the less they relied on obvious communication the better.

Daniel Levin slowly slipped the buckle from his seatbelt open, laid the pieces on the seat on each side of his legs, and made sure he had his seatmate's penknife ready. He had to take out the thug in his rear first (lucky for him they had all been taken off the plane, otherwise he might never have known about the threat behind him), then he would improvise from there. And Daniel had thought moving to the U.S. would allow him to avoid this. *Fat chance.*

0825 – Harrisburg, Pennsylvania

Detective Smith had stopped to refill his coffee mug and Elliott's Styrofoam cup. Now he was ready to continue pursuing the latest plot twist.

"So tell me about meeting your wife."

"She is an emergency room nurse. She was on a flight from Chicago and her aircraft was diverted into Harrisburg as a result of the attacks."

"Why was her flight diverted? Is it one of the hijack planes?" *That would have been good information to know half an hour ago.*

"Sorry, I forgot, the FAA grounded every flight in America after the attacks started."

Nevermind. "Really? I don't think they've ever done that before. For what, like all day?"

"I think it was for a couple of days. I don't remember exactly, but I think they did a staggered restart afterwards. It was weird seeing the pictures of the FAA radar screens with no planes on them."

"Go on."

"Anyway, she was on an American Airlines Flight out of

Chicago. They diverted into Harrisburg. She didn't know anything about the city and just went out to the Applebee's on Main Street to kill an evening. I ended up there and met her, just like that. We hit it off enough that she changed the train ticket back to Chicago she had bought for the next day. She still keeps the old train ticket."

"So you don't think she is going to be there tonight?"

"Not if her plane doesn't end up there, no way."

"You could go to Chicago and see her." Smith wasn't trying to play matchmaker. He just wanted to keep Graham talking, although the personal story was becoming very interesting.

"In Joliet? And do what? Knock on her door and say 'Hi, you've never met me before, but I know everything about you.'"

"Maybe you don't have to be that direct."

"But what else do I do? Loiter around until I get a chance to introduce myself, then try to invent a cover story about why a Harrisburg college professor is in Illinois? Then hope she is interested enough in me to start a relationship? Emotion across the country was running very high after the attacks. Maybe she just won't get hit with the same interest when she sees me this time. She had an on-and-off relationship with a doctor from her area at the time we met. Maybe that is suddenly going to start working again. It isn't like I'm that great a catch."

Detective Smith went to church with his family but wasn't deeply religious. "I guess you don't believe in Fate."

Elliott took a moment to think about that question: "It appears that the timeline I am on is altering, so it seems logical that the future I know is also gone. I have apparently already prevented one hijacking, assuming I am going to continue to live this life."

Smith was puzzled by the last part. "Excuse me?"

"Look, if I don't know how I got here, how do I know where I am going? I don't know what my tomorrow is going to be. I could wake up in your tomorrow with the new world I've created. I could wake up in 2014 with the new world I've created. I could wake up back in the next day of the old 2014 and simply think this was an intense dream. Maybe I'm going to wake up in this day over and over again, like *Groundhog Day*."

"You've heard of *Groundhog Day*?" Smith liked that movie. He was a big Andie McDowell fan.

"Dude, I'm from the future, not another planet."

"Don't call me 'dude'. So you were willing to sacrifice meeting your wife in order to prevent these attacks?"

"I don't think I gave it that much thought this morning. I mostly saw an opportunity and reacted. I wasn't thinking about what it could do to my personal future. I certainly don't think I would let 3,000 people die just to preserve the circumstances that I met my wife under."

What an interesting choice. "Well, we'll see how it works out."

0827 – Dulles International Airport, Washington, District of Columbia

Dulles Security Officer Ann Lemont was getting tired of listening to these clowns. In her experience, female authority figures and Arab men just did not go together well. She didn't care. She also knew perfectly well the way the two-faced game was played by the security bureaucracy; Profile Arab men, but don't appear to be profiling them. Our primary concern is the safety of the air passengers, but we don't want more complaints from Middle Eastern embassies. Technically, the five guys in the room had not broken any laws. But seriously, box cutters and brothers? They are obviously working together, and who takes box cutters with them when they travel? Interfering with their travel in any way was going to result in another complaint against her. On the other hand, isn't this what she was here for?

Fuck it.

Ann turned her authority figure voice back on. "Gentlemen, if you chose to travel, I am confiscating your weapons and will mail them at no cost to an address you designate. And…listen to me…settle down…thank you…and I will only allow three of you to travel on this aircraft. The others will be accommodated here at our expense and put on the next available flight opportunity to San Francisco."

And she thought the yelling had been bad when she walked in the room.

0828 – American Airlines Flight 11

Flight Attendant Karen Martin's heart skipped a beat when she saw four of the five men identified as a potential security threat rise almost in unison. The nearest two began moving toward her with an eerie calm. *Oh God, why?*

Daniel Levin felt his adrenalin surge through his body as he rocked ever so slightly forward to shift weight to his legs with the penknife clenched in his hand, using his peripheral vision to locate his adversary's jugular vein.

0829 – Dulles International Airport, Washington, District of Columbia

Hani Hanjour could scarcely control his fury over this insolent infidel, this woman, who dared transgress against the will of Allah and his own divine purpose. The problem wasn't figuring out which two team members to shed. The pallid skin and fear in the eyes of Majed and Khalid made it evident that they could no longer be counted on. The al-Hazmi brothers appeared calm and would carry each other through to the end. The problem was that three unarmed men couldn't possibly subdue an entire airplane of passengers and crew. They had decided that Ziad Jarrah could probably still carry out his mission short-handed, but that was with four armed men who had the advantage of surprise. The other problem he had warned against was that, by not launching all operations on airplanes from the same airport, there would be no possible way to know if all teams were committed to the attack. If only he knew for sure that the other operations were underway, he would certainly proceed with their mission no matter the likelihood of success or failure. But he did not know the status of any of the other teams. If the police had been given a tip about his team, it was possible the other missions were being interfered with as well. Frustrated at being so close to success without clearly knowing what to do, he continued to scream at the woman and her obviously hen-pecked assistants.

0830 – American Airlines Flight 11

Waleed al-Shehri knew that they had two important reasons to quickly secure the cockpit of the airplane. The first had been planned all along, to stop the crew's ability to communicate a distress message. The second that had emerged from the unexpected actions of the American security was the need to regain their weapons to enable them to control the passengers and crew. Through hand and eye gestures with Waid, they conceived and launched their hastily-hatched plan. It started with Waleed throwing an elbow at the stewardess's face to cut off her scream and brushing past her on his way to the cockpit, leaving Waid to finish with the attendants and anyone else in front who might cause trouble and follow him in.

Abdulaziz al-Omani took up position on the right side of the aircraft to seal the other route to the cockpit, ripping open the overhead bin to pull out a fire extinguisher he had spotted earlier to use as his weapon, either to club an individual or spray a crowd.

Mohammed Atta watched the Shehri brothers move toward the cockpit, which he considered the most important part of the operation, and felt his heart rise. *Maybe their mission was going to work despite all the problems Allah had seen fit to test them with*, he thought just as a flash of motion out of the corner of his eye coincided with a short, high-pitched scream.

Satam al-Suqami never knew what hit him. His jobs were to secure the left side of the aircraft from passengers or flight crew moving to the front, and warn the other mujahadeen in the unlikely event there was an air marshal on board. There were a couple of men in the seats in front of him, but he considered first-class passengers a minor hazard at best, and was confident that if necessary Atta would be able to contain them and the other first class passengers while the Shehri brothers captured the cockpit and recovered the team's weapons. Satam was more concerned with crewmembers and viewed the passengers as low threat in the crucial early stages of the operation. The Christians had been ingrained with not resisting hijackers, which meshed perfectly with their spineless nature. His primary concern was to secure some sort of usable weapon, so he was opening an overhead bin to find one when Daniel Levin drove the penknife into his neck, twisting as he withdrew it and plunging it in a second time, this time cracking into Satam's windpipe.

Atta was stunned to see a passenger stabbing Satam with a small knife. They had never anticipated an armed passenger from first class fighting back so quickly. The original plan had been for Atta to remain hidden until the other team members had secured the aircraft, then after the passengers had been herded into the back he would move into the cockpit. That would help disguise their numbers in the event of an attempt by the passengers to retake the aircraft, and create an inaccurate report by any passengers or crew who phoned the authorities from the aircraft. But they had all understood that he would be available as a reserve in case something went wrong during the takeover, which had become more likely once they had had their knives taken from them. He had been searching for a weapon, but quickly recovered and lunged back to tackle the new threat while shouting to Abdulaziz to help.

Pilot John Ogonowski heard Karen Martin's scream and turned around to see one of the assholes that security had pulled off the plane and subsequently put back on the plane entering the cockpit. Logan's security had also described the situation in detail before Amy had brought forward a small bag containing some knives. He was a military veteran and felt a meme from the past as he had pulled out a nice-looking Swiss Army knife and placed it on the instrument panel in front of him "just in case." However, they had mistakenly neglected to secure the cockpit door. Now he tried to grab for the knife, but the assailant was already pinning his arm at his side as he tried to reach for the knife, then picked it up himself and plunged it into John's arm.

Daniel Levin was confident he had disabled the first goon as Atta crashed into him, with both men bouncing heavily off the mid-plane flight attendant station and onto the floor. In the process Daniel was able to wrench his knife arm free and began slashing wildly at the new threat.

First Officer Thomas McGuinness was a military veteran like his senior pilot. The two of them had discussed the emerging security situation with a similar perspective on the potential problems. Nonetheless, Tom had been amused to watch his older companion take one of the knives and place it within arm's reach. Now he found himself frantically reaching down to find another edged device from the bag of confiscated weapons, while hearing his partner cry out as he watched the attacker wrestle the knife free and stab his partner in the arm.

Abdulaziz Omani turned the corner around the crew station against a background of screaming passengers to see an absolute mess. Satam was down, blood spurting through his hands from wounds in his neck and gurgling incoherently. Atta was also on the floor trying to fight against a passenger who was slashing at his face and hands with a small knife. *How did he get a knife?* Abdulaziz swung the unfamiliar fire extinguisher clumsily, trying to smash Atta's attacker in the head.

Daniel saw the next Arab out of the corner of his eye, detected the arm motion with weapon and perceiving this as the greater threat, even though he had not quite taken out the man beneath him, released him and was able to roll far enough away to take the blow on his left shoulder and instinctively thrust back with the penknife.

At the front of the cabin, Waid al-Shehri had sent a judicious kick into the flight attendant's abdomen, then turned to the left, ripped the coat rack bar out of the closet, and moved toward the cockpit to help his brother subdue the pilots.

Waleed's hand had slipped off the now-bloody knife while he was trying to pull it out of the pilot's arm and he was wrestling with him to regain control when he felt a searing pain along his right side.

Thomas McGuinness wasn't thrilled with a box cutter as his weapon and wished he had been as paranoid as his partner before the attack started, but all he could do now was keep slashing at the attacker draped over the Captain and hope for the best.

Abdulaziz Omani ignored the sharp pain in his leg and brought the fire extinguisher down a second time on the passenger who had just stabbed him from below. This time he was able to score a glancing blow to the infidel's head.

Daniel rolled off to the side and looked up dully as he saw the third man preparing to smash him again. He tried to will his arms up to block the blow, but he had been stunned by the last hit and realized that this was the end. His last thought was *They didn't get me without a fight.*

Abdulaziz brought the fire extinguisher down three more times to make sure this troublesome infidel (and Jew at that) was truly dead.

Waid entered the cockpit and saw his brother wrestling with both pilots, blood already covering all three of them, and instinctively chose the younger one as his target. He turned toward him and tried to swing the coat rack bar at him but it glanced off the ceiling instead, demonstrating why all of the groups had favored edged weapons over blunt instruments while planning a takeover attempt inside the cramped confines of an airplane. Waid gripped the coat rack bar to use it as a battering ram, then moved closer and began thrusting it at the co-pilot.

Thomas McGuinness took a glancing blow to the head from the coatrack, but not enough to disorient him as he moved to grapple with this latest assailant and seized the opportunity to slash him as well.

Waleed was in great pain from the cuts he had received from the co-pilot, but quickly moved to help Waid and tried to break the stubborn man's grip on his brother's weapon so Waid could finish subduing him.

With Waleed's help, Waid finally pulled the coat rack free and resumed thrusting it at him. It really wasn't a heavy enough bar to inflict disabling damage on the target, but repeated blows were sapping the energy from his opponent and with Waleed's help, he was finally rewarded by seeing the man slump back in his seat unconscious. In their exhilaration, both Waid and Waleed forgot about the older man.

John Ogonowski gritted his teeth while freeing the knife from his arm. He turned back toward his former attacker, summoned a surge of strength from within himself, and plunged the knife into the man's side, pushing through and penetrating his kidney.

Waleed's cry reminded Waid there was another person in the cockpit and he turned the coat rack on the older pilot. Now with more room he could change from thrusting to partial swings with the coat rack bar. He got in three swings before he heard Waleed feebly say, "Stop brother! Remember we cannot kill the pilots until Mohammed tells us."

Waid stopped, still breathing heavily from the struggle, stared at the unconscious pilots and gave his brother a quizzical look.

Waleed knew what he was thinking. "I don't know how to fly either!" *Where was Mohammed Atta? He should have been in the cockpit by now. Did something go wrong in the cabin?* Neither Waleed nor Waid knew how to fly. The automatic pilot must have been engaged by one of the pilots so at least they were still in the air, but they needed Atta to do anything other than that.

0832 – New York, New York

Moira Smith was in the 13th Precinct headquarters when they received a call from their borough headquarters that a credible threat of a potential terrorist attack had been received on their phone line and corroborated by the FBI. All precincts were to be prepared to provide support for orderly evacuation of key government and other facilities throughout the city if necessary.

Moira was assigned by her lieutenant to proceed to the World Trade Center. She obeyed with her customary enthusiasm and quickly headed out with the other assigned officers to the motor pool for the trip there.

0833 – Dulles International Airport, Washington, District of Columbia

Hani Hanjour stormed out of the Dulles holding room, still cursing and threatening the security officials. He was frustrated that he did not know the status of the other teams, frustrated that they had been mere minutes from success, frustrated that he had been beaten by a woman. He was also uncertain what to do next because in their overconfidence they had failed to establish a safe house to retreat to in the event of being forced to abort the mission. As he walked by Khalid and Nawaf he mouthed "Fundook" (hotel) and they both had nodded back. Hopefully the whole team would reassemble at the Residence

Inn where they had stayed the night before. If any of the other teams succeeded in carrying out their missions, it would only be a matter of time before the infidels traced their investigation back to him and his team. They also needed to use a rental car rather than hired transportation in the event they needed to quickly evacuate the hotel. Fortunately he had travelled to Ontario two years earlier and vaguely knew the area. The team might be reliant on his familiarity by nightfall.

Ann Lemont had been a bit surprised when none of the suspects had chosen to board the flight. Even more interesting to her, she had had to offer to refund their ticket money to them before they even seemed to think about it. *I guess you guys can't have anything that important waiting for you in LA,* she thought sarcastically. She told her assistants not to hand the men their weapons back until they had watched the suspects exit the airport doors and then continue to observe them until they departed the grounds. She also intended to recommend to the airport chief of security that photos of the men be distributed to all security personnel. Ann figured that she was about to have another round of arduous complaint and inquiry boards to deal with in the aftermath of the suspect's inevitable complaints. *I'm just trying to do my job, dammit.* As she headed back to her office, she suspected that the FBI was also going to want to know about the encounter she had just had.

0834 – American Airlines Flight 11

Abdulaziz al-Omari was in the cabin wiping the blood from Atta's face. Circumstances had forced Atta to reveal himself sooner than planned. This had been necessary, but it left them in a precarious situation. Even though Abdulaziz had also done some flight simulator training, Atta was by far the superior pilot of the two men. The plan was that if necessary, Abdulaziz could serve as copilot for Atta. But he did not understand enough of flying, navigation and communications to get their airplane to the World Trade Center by himself. That meant that in order to fully succeed they were reliant on Atta to carry out their mission. As he worked on Atta, he could see at a glance that Satam's condition was far worse. The hoarse exhalations and clamminess of his skin indicated that he was dying from the severe neck wounds inflicted on him by the attacking passenger. How were the al-Shehri brothers doing? Why hadn't one of them come back to tell them the cockpit was secured? The plane had gone through some minor gyrations, but right now they seemed to be flying straight and level. He wanted to check, but right now Atta was the most important person on the airplane.

0835 – Newark International Airport, Newark, New Jersey

Ziad Jarrah was certain that something must have gone wrong. Surely they had been betrayed by another team member, or even one of the people who had supported their planning and logistics. The uncertainty was the worst part; any wrong move could jeopardize not only their mission, but potentially all the others. He wished he could simply abort the mission and walk away, but it was too late for that now. He was about to conclude that they were destined for failure when he felt United Flight 93 beginning to back away from the terminal.

0836 – Boston, Massachusetts

Air Traffic Controller Ed Zwick saw that American Airlines

Flight 11 had failed to turn to maintain its assigned air corridor heading, and now they had blown through the checkpoint entirely and were leaving the area. Things like this did happen, so Ed still treated it as a minor error on the part of the pilots.

Ed keyed his microphone, "American 11, this is Boston Center, I show you well to the left of course. Turn right immediately heading 260 to avoid traffic south of your position."

0837 – Harrisburg, Pennsylvania

Detective Smith pursed his lips ever so slightly as he slowly put down the phone and stared at Elliott Graham.

"They just pulled another group off a plane at Dulles. Five Arab men, knives, the whole works. Who the hell are you?"

Elliott saw that the detective had finally lost any hint of maliciousness or sarcasm in his tone. "Are they boarding?"

Coming right back at me, this guy is persistent. "Nope, it sounds like they declined."

That was some relief for Graham. Maybe he was starting to make some progress after all. "That leaves one group, and it is the group with only four members. You can tell your people to stop searching for planes with five Arabs."

"We have half of America acting on your tip, and now you're changing it?"

"Yes."

Smith did not think making a change to his random terrorist alert tip this soon was going to go over very well with the rest of the law enforcement community. "You're that sure?"

"Absolutely. Have you already forgotten the name of the guy who killed JFK?"

Smith had not. He was having a hard time reconciling a guy who claimed to be from the future being so attuned to pop culture and current events. Maybe it was just habit from a lifetime of watching science-fiction movies where people moved centuries or more through time. Graham had merely placed himself a pedestrian thirteen years in the future. Smith tried to remind himself that time travel was ludicrous as he picked the phone back up.

"Get me the FBI, please."

0838 – American Airlines Flight 11

Mohammed Atta had at last been sufficiently revived by Abdulaziz to make his way unsteadily down the aisle of the aircraft toward the cockpit. He moved inside to see Waid tending to his brother Waleed. He looked and saw both pilots slumped over in the chairs. Yallah, was no one flying the plane? The al-Shehri brothers were supposed to keep at least one pilot conscious while he took control of flying the aircraft, ideally until he was ready to make the final approach. With no transmissions and probably flying off course, air control was going to get curious by now, if they had not already been trying to contact the plane. With great effort, Atta was able to pull the limp form of the copilot out of the right seat and place himself in the chair. He placed the headset on and heard an air traffic controller calling the flight to ascertain their status.

To Atta the situation seemed little short of disastrous. Satam was dead or dying. Waleed was down hard and unable to help in any substantial way. Abdulaziz had a minor leg wound from the passenger with whom they had fought. Atta himself had also had his face cut quite badly during his struggle with that damned Jew from first class. Waid was now the only unwounded member of their team. They were facing a sullen mob with only two muscle hijackers left for crowd control, including his contingency co-pilot Abdulaziz. They were behind schedule, there had already been some sort of tip about this mission to the Americans, and they did not know if any of the other mujahedeen were conducting their operations. If they were, it would increase the chance of outside interference with their mission.

On the other hand, he was now in control of the airplane. They had done it starting with no weapons and an ad hoc plan that did not foresee the fiercest resistance coming from first class. They had also regained their weapons and temporarily subdued the passengers. The operation was not yet a failure by any means, and could still be carried to a successful conclusion. Allah was most beneficent to his faithful warriors. His will be done.

Atta fairly shouted over to his fellow teammember, "Waid, pay less attention to Waleed and get this pilot out of here. Then go into the back and help Abdulaziz control the others; the passengers are very unruly. Quickly!"

0839

Pilot John Ogonowski roused slightly from unconsciousness. He was groggy and in great pain, but managed to reset the cockpit transmitter to a setting that would allow the controllers on the ground to hear everything that was being said in the cockpit.

Mohammad Atta did not notice as he was still dealing with Waid. He turned off the plane's transponder (mistakenly thinking the ground controllers would no longer be able to track them; radar could still track them, just less effectively) and then came onto what he thought was the airplane intercom and said, "We have some planes. Just stay quiet and you'll be okay. We're returning to the airport."

0840 – Newark International Airport, Newark, New Jersey

Lee Chang had not been told by his bosses what Newark departure times he should begin searching for, so he had played it safe and gone all the way back to the first flight of the day. He had found nothing so far until he got to United Flight 93, when he came up with four distinctly Arab names, but not five. Just to make sure, he looked at the flight's destination: San Francisco, not Los Angeles. Close on both counts, but not a hit. Lee shrugged his shoulders and moved to the next manifest.

0840:30 – Boston, Massachusetts

Ed Zwick was the Boston Air Route Traffic Control Center air traffic controller who had been transmitting routine instructions to aircraft in his zone of responsibility including American Airlines Flight 11 when that flight had ceased responding. He tried unsuccessfully several times to regain contact with the aircraft to no avail, and now watched as their tracking blip disappeared off his screen, meaning that their transponder had been turned off. Then he noticed that the aircraft cockpit transmitter had been turned on. He stopped transmitting and listened in time to hear a voice with a foreign accent:

"Nobody move. Everything will be okay. If you try to make any moves, you'll endanger yourself and the airplane. Just stay quiet."

Ed turned and saw his immediate supervisor, David Sierra. "Sir, I believe that we have a potential hijacking on American Airlines Flight 11. It's the same plane that they pulled some passengers off of earlier and confiscated weapons which they were carrying."

Sierra interjected, "They were allowed back on the aircraft?"

"Yes, sir. They hadn't done anything illegal at that time so airport security probably didn't want another complaint about targeting Arab men on their hands. The aircraft is no longer on its assigned flight path, is not responding to my contact attempts, has turned off its transponder, and I hear a voice with a foreign accent talking to the passengers. He probably doesn't know that I can hear him. I would recommend that we notify the FAA immediately, including the FCOC at Cape Cod. And the controller for that other flight that took on Arabs probably needs to be notified."

Sierra looked over at Leslie Wharton, the Boston FAA Center military liaison, who had just walked in and was being brought up to speed on the situation. He nodded and said "We need to tell NORAD about the problem and get some military jets scrambled to intercept, probably from Otis."

Dan said, "Okay Leslie, I'll start working it up the FAA, you get a hold of the Air Force and give them a heads up that they'll probably get a call."

Leslie responded, "Yes, sir."

0841 – Boston, Massachusetts

American Airlines Flight 11 had begun turning south as Boston Center called the FAA Air Traffic Control System Command Center in Herndon, Virginia and notified them that it believed Flight 11 had been hijacked and was heading toward New York's airspace. The Command Center established a conference call between Boston, New York and Cleveland Centers in the event Flight 11 strayed out of Boston's airspace and into that of an adjacent zone.

0841:30 – Otis Air Force Base, Massachusetts

Otis Air National Guard Base in Massachusetts was home to the 102nd Fighter Wing. The 102nd had a distinguished history that included making frequent Cold War interceptions of long-range Soviet bombers and then "escorting" them to Cuba. The Cold War was long gone, but the 102nd's mission of aerospace defense of the United States continued, and a limited number of aircraft and pilots were maintained in a constant state of readiness on the ready ramp, fueled and armed.

Air Force Lieutenant Colonel Gerry Wertz (call sign Lizard) and Major Steve Walker (Chop) were the on-call duty pilots when a Federal Aviation Administration call from the Cape Cod Facility Calls Operation Center came in to their unit operations center. The superintendent of aviation management listened and quickly handed the telephone to Lizard. Cape Cod told Lizard that a call from NEADS could be expected soon and that an order for a fighter intercept of a potentially hijacked aircraft over the continental U.S. was likely. He immediately got on the radio to Chop and told him to suit up and get ready for a scramble call.

0842 – Newark International Airport, Newark, New Jersey

Captain Jason Dahl pushed the throttles forward and United Airlines Flight 93 began its takeoff roll from Newark International Airport forty-one minutes behind schedule. In seat 1B, Ziad Jarrah watched the ground fall out from beneath them and relaxed for the first time that day. Allah Akbar!

0842:30 – American Airlines Flight 11

Mohammed Atta sensed the hostages in the back getting restless and again clicked on the intercom and addressed the passengers and crew of AA Flight 11. "Nobody move, please. We are going back to the airport. Don't try to make any stupid moves."

Ed Zwick was listening intently and promptly relayed the gist of the conversation to his supervisory chain.

0843

David Angell was ready to act. He had been surprised by the hijacking even though he had seen the suspicious-looking characters get pulled off of American Airlines Flight 11 and then put back on. David was a well-known name in Hollywood, where his award-winning career in comedy writing and producing had run through the successful television programs *Cheers* and *Wings*, and he was now riding high as executive producer of *Frasier*. He was tired from the family wedding he and his wife Lynn had hosted at their home in Rhode Island, but he was now on full-adrenaline alert. The assault by the hijackers had happened and been over before he could react. He was sure that the hijackers had not expected to have one of their team killed and two more injured, and he saw that only two hijackers were left to control them as they were being moved toward the back of the plane. The hijackers were probably vulnerable to a counter-attack right now. David wasn't as young as he used to be if this turned into hand-to-hand combat, but he sure didn't feel like being stuck for three weeks roasting on this airplane while it sat on a Caribbean tarmac. After gently pushing Lynn into the crush of passengers moving back, he looked around and spotted a similar sense of resolve in the eyes of an alert, robust-looking passenger across the middle row of seats.

Jeffrey Coombs fully understood the look from the older gentleman. *Let's do something!* he thought. He was amazed at the amount of blood splattered around the cabin from the men who had been struggling, including the passenger who had fought three hijackers and injured them all, including one who appeared to be dead. Jeff's passion for outdoor activity might have seemed like an incongruity alongside his day job as a computer security analyst. He did know that he had had enough of being pushed around by the hijackers. Jeff figured their best chance to retake the aircraft would be before the hijackers could really solidify their control of the plane and passengers. He decided to create a diversion of looking in overhead bins, then would use a suitcase as a shield to rush the hijacker coming toward him. Maybe they would even get some help from the other passengers. Anything was better than just doing nothing.

0844 – United Airlines Flight 175

Pilot Victor Saracini was being brought up to speed on the events occurring on American Airlines Flight 11 and responded to the flight controller: "Copy that. I intend to divert to Pittsburgh International with an en route descent to a straight-on approach. If these guys are the real deal and try to take over our airplane, I want to delay them figuring out what we are doing for as long as possible. I intend to stop the moment I can pull off the runway and shut down the engines on the spot. Request current winds and landing runway at Pittsburgh."

"Copy Flight 175: there will be FBI agents waiting for you when you arrive in Pittsburgh. I'm turning you over to Pittsburgh now. Good luck, Captain."

"Thanks, Center." Vic glanced over at Mike Horrocks before toggling the microphone. "Mr. Fangman, come in, please."

Fangman was glad to hear from his captain. "Yes, sir."

"There has been a hijacking on another plane out of Boston. We're diverting to Pittsburgh. We'll descend slowly to try and keep our guests in the dark for as long as possible. Don't tell any of the passengers, but keep them away from the suspects. We don't need a hostage situation. Pass a note to the air marshal and let him know about the hijacking and our intention to divert. Make sure he knows that the FBI is supposed to have agents on the ground to meet us when we land."

"Yes, sir."

"Captain out." Vic turned back to his copilot. "Ain't this some shit, Mike?"

"FUBAR Vic. Why did they let them on the plane in the first place?"

"I agree. Cut off all communications for the back of the plane. No use getting a panic started if someone in the cabin gets a call from their wife telling them about the hijacking. Let's just be ready to put this thing on the ground the moment we have to, okay?"

"Copy, Vic."

Saracini toggled the microphone. "Pittsburgh Approach, this is United Flight 175 out of Boston, diverting to Pittsburgh International with a request for assistance."

0847 – Harrisburg, Pennsylvania

Smith's desk phone rang at last and he picked it up and

listened. Elliott saw him sit up even straighter as the conversation went on.

"I'll be damned." Smith put down the phone and stared at Elliott. "Flight 11 out of Boston has just been hijacked."

Graham felt an adrenaline surge that was so powerful that it left his hands shaking. *Dammit! How had he failed? What could he have done differently? Was the day and all its tragedy going to play out just like he remembered despite his efforts? Were the events of 9/11 fated to happen? Maybe the other hijackers were boarding the other planes even now.*

Graham asked Smith, "How did it happen?"

"I don't know. It sounds like someone turned on the cockpit voice box and the FAA is overhearing their conversation." Smith shook his head in amazement. Even without weapons, the attackers had not only made the hijacking attempt, but had improbably succeeded. *Who are these guys?* He thought to himself.

As Graham began speaking, Smith realized that he had in fact said the last part out loud. "These guys are real hard cases, Detective. They're suicides…like I said before." Elliott added the last part for passive aggressive emphasis.

The story still didn't make sense to Smith. "Why would they leave a pilot in the cockpit if they are suicides? A pilot who isn't part of their plot isn't going to knowingly crash the airplane."

"I don't remember. I think only one hijacker in each group is trained to fly. Maybe they will use the pilot until they get close to the target and then kill him. He could make their radio calls and deflect suspicion from the ground controllers. The pilots don't know that these guys are suicides. Everyone today is going to assume these guys are just hijackers and the safest course is to cooperate. Hey look, are you guys doing anything or not?"

"Calm down, Mr. Graham. I already called in your specific tip that we are down to one four-member hijacking team. I also intend to call the FBI back and recommend that they detain the members of the two other teams that were uncovered, assuming they aren't doing this already."

"How about evacuating the World Trade Center? That is where Atta is going to try and take his plane."

"I'll call the FBI again and recommend an evacuation. Is that fair enough?"

Elliott was frustrated, but realized he certainly couldn't ask for more than Detective Smith was doing. This was turning out to be a lot harder than he thought it would be. Why was a schoolteacher from Harrisburg the man who had to try to stop 9/11? "Fair enough."

0848 – American Airlines Flight 11

Abdulaziz al-Omari was trying to go about the task of herding the passengers and unnecessary crewmembers into the back of the plane with help from the shaken Waid working the other aisle. He knew this was not an ideal situation. The plan had been to have two mujahedeen working an aisle to protect each other. Even having one man in the middle as a reserve would have helped intimidate the passengers into submission, but Waleed was not in a condition to assist them. With only one operative and no one available behind him, the passengers might be emboldened to try and rush one or even both of them. He was annoyed to see one passenger near the front who was rooting around in one of the overhead bins.

"Yallah. Move to the back of the airplane now!"

"Please don't hurt me!" Jeffrey Coombs tried to sound

pathetic.

0848:30 – United Airlines Flight 175

Jeremy Blivens read the note surreptitiously handed him by one of the United Airlines Flight 175 attendants along with a glass of water.

Hijacking in another aircraft. Pilot diverting to Pittsburgh. Slow glide path.

Fan-freakin-tastic! Jeremy thought. He had no one but himself to blame. He could have kept them off the plane, but he didn't feel like getting behind in the game of office politics. On the other hand, he might have just been handed the opportunity to jump to the head of the class. But in the meantime, he needed to stay ahead of the suspects, whom he still didn't know for sure intended to seize the aircraft. Three of them without weapons meant their best option would be to try to rush him, but the narrow aisles meant they would not all be able to reach him at once. Assuming that they all decided to attack, there was always the faint chance one or two might chicken out. The guy in the back window location seemed to be the least enthusiastic. Now Jeremy was glad he had selected the seat he did. He unbuckled his seat belt and opened his jacket.

0849 – American Airlines Flight 11

Jeffrey Coombs had found a nice carryon; soft enough to absorb a knife, but with some heft to it as well to allow him to push it into the nearest hijacker. He really did not have much of a plan other than to get close to the nearest hijacker and keep moving forward. He tried to look scared as he moved closer to the hijacker.

"Yallah! Move!"

Coombs lunged the final two steps with the suitcase thrust in front of him and pushed as his arm was slashed by the box cutter.

Waid turned to see a solidly-built passenger attack Abdulaziz. He started to move around to the other aisle then felt a dull thud as a laptop computer bounced off his head. He staggered back and tripped over Satam's body, falling heavily to the ground as a grey-haired passenger landed on top of him with fists flailing.

Albert Dominguez saw that both hijackers were under attack. The Aussie baggage-handler screamed "Let's get them!" as he followed the first passenger to the hijacker lying on the ground and began kicking his head.

Abdulaziz was being forced back by the passenger with the suitcase even though he had cut him at least twice. He saw Waid down on the ground with two passengers working him over and others beginning to move towards both of them. Abdulaziz knew he should try to help Waid, but instead in that moment he panicked, turned and began fleeing towards the front of the airplane, pursued closely by his hostages-turned-attackers.

David Angell had broken his left hand and taken a couple of slight slash wounds, but he was able to roll off the hijacker through a thicket of legs kicking the now-defenseless form. He was also grateful to see other passengers moving past him toward the cabin. He shouted, "Don't let them lock the cabin door!"

0850 – Otis Air Force Base, Massachusetts

The squadron commander at Otis AFB had asked for

permission from NEADS to launch his alert fighters. They responded by ordering the weapons team commander to place the fighters on "battle stations." This resulted in a warning siren sounding at Otis that sent Lizard and Chop sprinting out to their F-15C fighters to go through an abbreviated pre-flight check in anticipation of a scramble order.

Even though the 102nd was an Air Force National Guard unit, Lizard's work flying fighters for them was actually a full-time gig. He relished every opportunity to get in the cockpit of the fast and powerful F-15 air superiority fighter plane. He had picked up his call sign by his passion for the outdoors, running and hiking outdoors with his long, gangly frame gliding endlessly across the countryside.

Chop had wanted to fly ever since he was a young boy. He had flown for a number of years as a full time, or active duty pilot, for the Air Force before joining the Air National Guard and being assigned to Otis the previous year. Chop was marked for greatness back in basic training when he earned the title "Big Bad Basic."

Chop had originally been scheduled to be flight lead, but while they were preparing to go Lizard asked him if he had ever been in a hijack situation before, to which Chop responded negatively.

"I have." Lizard responded. "A long time ago, I intercepted a hijacked civilian jet."

Chop thought about that and said, "Okay, you take the lead. I'll be Number Two."

0851 – American Airlines Flight 11

Mohammed Atta had been concentrating on flying the aircraft, so even though he heard some noise from behind the cabin, he was still startled by Abdulaziz rushing into the cockpit and attempting to slam the door shut. However, Abdulaziz was unable to do so before a bloody passenger pushed the door open, with the sound of others close behind. Atta saw in a flash that Abdulaziz would not be able to fend off the passengers. Curse the Fates! If it hadn't been for that damned Jew from first class ambushing them and killing Satam, they probably would have been able to keep control of the aircraft for the whole mission, not just seize it temporarily. This meant they were not going to reach the target. He had prepared himself for this contingency. If the mission would not succeed, that didn't mean he couldn't take this plane load of infidels with him. And he could do one more thing in case even this would not be his destiny. He reached toward the throttles and hurriedly changed some nearby levers and switches, then began nosing the aircraft towards what would be a fatal dive.

David Angell felt his balance going and knew what it meant. "They're crashing the plane! Get to the pilot's seat now, now, *now!*"

0852

The steepening descent angle of Flight 11 acted like an instinctive stimulant to John Ogonowski. He vaguely remembered where he was and could also hear discordant screaming behind him and understood that the passengers were attempting to retake the aircraft. He summoned his strength, set his feet, grabbed the control yoke in front of him and pulled back, fighting against the hijacker seated next to him.

The increased angle in conjunction with his grappling with

a passenger caused Abdulaziz to fall back into Mohammed Atta and briefly knocked Atta's hands from the yoke. Even as Atta grabbed it again he felt another passenger striking him with a heavy object. From the corner of his eye he vaguely saw Abdulaziz falling to his knees under a vicious attack from two other passengers, looking as if it was happening in a dream far away. All their planning, preparation, and sacrifice would end up going for naught. Atta had hoped to leave behind a name that would strike fear into the infidels for generations, but now he knew he would be little more than a footnote. Emotionlessly he resigned himself to his destiny.

"Forgive us, Allah, we have failed you."

0853

Jeffrey Coombs was in a bloodlust rage and continued to strike the Arab long after he had stopped moving until Albert Dominguez yelled, "I think you can stop now mate, the guy's brains are coming out. Pull him out of there and get in the chair."

Coombs' mind began to come back into focus. "I don't know how to fly."

"Just get in and get this thing back to level. Can you do that?"

"Probably, but someone else is going to have to bring us down. How do the pilots look?"

Coombs had already seen their copilot on the way in and decided at a glance that he was too badly injured to be able to help. The older pilot, who he had seen fighting the hijacker for control of the plane, was now slumped back in the chair. "I think we can get this one revived, but maybe not anytime soon. We need any help we can get from a passenger who knows anything about flying. At this point I'll take a kid who flies on his home computer."

"I'm on it." Dominquez turned and shouted to the crowd of panting, sobbing, even laughing people behind him, "Does anyone here know how to fly a plane?"

"I'll try," said Charles Jones.

The ebullient Dominquez responded, "Good enough. You're hired, mate! We need help now! And we need a doctor too!"

"Okay. Let me in," said Jones. As he moved toward the cockpit he noticed a deafening silence and asked, "Did you guys shut off the engines?"

0854 – Harrisburg, Pennsylvania

Detective Smith asked Elliott Graham, "So what will you do if you change your future and don't meet your wife this evening?"

"I don't know," Graham responded. "I haven't really thought about it. I guess I have to try and contact her. But If I can't win her heart again, what kind of life will I end up with? Life with her and the kids is what I've known for over a decade, and I liked it. Maybe it will feel as if she died, and I was in mourning. It is hard to imagine myself just going out on a date with someone else next weekend."

He wasn't exactly trying to be a troublemaker, but Detective Smith couldn't help but jump in, "There isn't anyone you are excited about having a second chance with? Not even a little bit?"

Interesting: Elliott was no different than other humans who harbored do-over thoughts that they knew would never come to fruition, but being confronted with precisely that opportunity, he was surprised to instead fiercely realize how much he wanted to hang on to what he had. And yet, that was a nice smile he had gotten from the Laundromat girl this morning. A nice smile…forget it. "I don't really see myself doing it. It will feel weird, like I'm cheating on Tiffany and betraying my whole family, you know?"

Smith could see his point, although he had a couple of private fantasies he thought he wouldn't mind seeing play out. *Maybe it looks different when the opportunity is actually in front of you; the fantasy carries far less risk.* "I guess. So will it be worth it to you? All that you may be sacrificing? After all, if you win, no one will know, right?"

"I guess not." *That's the idea.*

"So what is a win to you?"

Elliott hadn't thought about it that way, but the answer seemed pretty clear. "Preventing three thousand people from dying today."

"So you might wake up tomorrow morning sentenced to relive an uncertain future?"

"Or I could wake up with no knowledge of what I have done. Or I could wake up in 2014 with the new future I have created. I really don't know, and I haven't given it a great deal of thought since I woke up this morning and figured out that I was in a different decade from the one I went to bed in last night with an opportunity in front of me."

Smith was at least finding conversation with Graham more entertaining than the normal suspect. Actually, usual was probably a better word to describe suspects than normal. He asked Graham, "So what makes you different from *Groundhog Day*?"

Elliott thought about that for a long moment and said, "The point of the movie was a man making an ordinary day extraordinary. I'm trying to make an extraordinary day ordinary."

0854:30 – One World Trade Center

Scoop Esposito was in his Cantor-Fitzgerald office when he heard the building evacuation protocol. He recognized it the moment it began, because this was not the first time he had heard it. Scoop had been working here on February 23rd, 1993 when Arab terrorists had parked a truck containing over 1300 pounds of explosives underneath Tower One, with the explosion killing six people. Scoop and a colleague had helped lead a pregnant woman out of the building on that occasion. The worst part to Scoop had been walking all the way down from the 104th floor.

You've got to be kidding me! It took me two hours to climb down last time, and I was a younger man back then. What could be worse than a truck bomb? Alien invasion? Locusts?

0855 – American Airlines Flight 11

Charles Jones had finally made his way into the cabin of the plane and sat in the pilot's chair. Jones was a Hoosier who had graduated from the United States Air Force Academy and eventually gone on to become a manned spaceflight engineer at NASA, one of the dream assignments for a "Zoomie," as USAFA cadets were known. He had been scheduled to fly on Space Shuttle mission number STS-71-B, but that mission had been cancelled after the explosion of the *Challenger* in January of 1986. He had retired from the Air Force as a Colonel and was living in Massachusetts where he was now hard at work pursuing his second love of scuba diving. He turned to the bloodied man seated in the co-pilot's chair next to him struggling to keep the plane level. "I'm Chuck."

Coombs was thrilled with the reinforcement. "I'm Jeff."

Chuck noticed the blood on Coombs, not to mention just about everything else in the cockpit. "How's your arm?"

"It hurts, but I'll live."

"Yeah, but are you going to pass out? I need someone to work the radios now, because unless you did it, I think the hijackers shut down our engines and we need to get them restarted pretty quick." In the meantime, Chuck looked in the area around the throttles and found the engine start levers, and saw that they were currently in the cutoff position. "Hold on, I think I found the problem."

"What?"

"I think they turned off these levers down here. Lemme give this a try." He reached down and pushed the levers to the full on position.

Nothing.

Chuck cycled them down and back up a second time.

Nothing.

"Crap, that isn't doing anything. Okay Jeff, let's see if we can find someone to talk to."

"How do I do it?"

"Push that button under the green numbers and the word "active." Then make a call and see if anyone responds. Meanwhile, hand me that little book, it's the flight manual."

Jeff promptly complied. *At least this guy sounds organized, that has to be a good thing.* "Okay. So you're a pilot?"

"Ah, not exactly. Spaceflight engineer."

"You mean like NASA?"

"Yep. Let's get going, we need power fast and it looks like we're losing about two thousand feet per minute."

"Is that a lot?"

"Yep." This was going to be a difficult job. At least the sky was clear. He wouldn't have to fight the weather on top of all their other challenges.

Jeff had little idea of what proper radio protocol was, but he did know one word that would get everyone's attention. "Mayday! Mayday! Mayday! This is Flight..." *what was their flight number again? My ticket is back at my seat.* That seemed funny to him now. He had actually paid to be in this situation.

Chuck broke in, "Its 11."

"Thanks. Mayday, this is American Flight 11! We just retook the aircraft from our hijackers but the engines are out. Can anyone hear me?"

0856 – Boston, Massachusetts

Ed Zwick was both gratified and dismayed. Now he understood why the plane had lost contact with him and gone off course. "American Airlines Flight 11, this is Boston Center, it's good to hear you! Say again your emergency please."

Jeff responded, "We just took the aircraft from our hijackers, but the engines are out."

"Where are your airline pilots?"

"The hijackers cut them up. Neither one is conscious. No one else has said they are a pilot."

Ed asked, "Do you know why the engines are out? Is there any structural damage? Please visually inspect the cockpit and the actual engines."

Jeff looked at Chuck who said, "I already did that. Tell him I think the hijackers shut down the engines before we retook the plane. When I got here the engine start levers were off. I turned them on a couple of times, but nothing happened."

Jeff said, "We already checked for damage and didn't see anything; we think the asshole hijackers shut them down. The engine start levers were off when we got in: we tried to turn them on but nothing happened."

Ed knew he needed a pilot as soon as possible to talk to American Airlines Flight 11, but in the meantime he said, "Okay, you need to turn them back off. You probably need to do a complete engine restart procedure. Turn the engine start levers off first and then look over your heads for a switch on the upper instrument panel for your power."

Chuck stopped flipping through the checklists, turned the engine start levers back off, then looked up at the instrument panel and saw a switch labeled "ENG START." "Got it." He looked at the switches, but they were in the "AUTO" position. He glanced at the altimeter and saw that they were passing below 6,000 feet. "Okay, tell them the switches are turned on. Nothing is happening."

Jeff relayed to Ed, "Power's on, nothing is happening."

"You just turned them on?"

"No, they've been on all the time. Do you want me to cycle them off and on?"

In the meantime Chuck had found the checklist for engine startup, scanned through it, then flipped the left engine switch to the checklist position.

Nothing.

Chuck tried it again.

Nothing.

Chuck glanced at the altimeter: 5000 feet.

"It's not working. Trying the right engine now." Chuck turned off the left engine switch and turned on the one for the right engine.

Nothing.

Chuck tried it again.

Nothing.

4000 feet.

Jeff relayed this info to Ed Zwick.

Ed said, "Okay, an airborne startup is probably going to be a bit different. Skip on down the checklist."

Chuck was complying as he glanced at the dial and saw the final setting FLT for flight. "I might have it."

"Okay 11, but I have your altitude at about 3500 feet, so you're going to need to lower your landing gear pretty soon and be ready to put down wherever you are."

Chuck had flipped the dial and tried the right engine.

Nothing.

Chuck tried again.

Nothing.

3000 feet.

Ed broke in, "Flight 11, you need to deploy your landing gear and flaps now. Do you know how?"

Chuck responded, "Yes, I do. Extending landing gear and flaps now." He hadn't really paid much attention to the terrain below. Now he glanced down and wasn't too happy with what he saw; the ground was fairly broken with a lot of trees. There was a road running to the left of their flight path, but now they were too low to make it there. "Jeff, pick out a spot for us to put down: the longer and flatter, the better." Then he turned on the intercom. "Everyone put on seat belts now!"

2500 feet.

Ed said, "We're vectoring emergency vehicles to your likely landing area." Now he knew he couldn't wait any longer for a pilot and just decided to do it the fast way. Switching over to emergency frequency, he called, "All aircraft, all aircraft, I have an American Airlines 767 Flight 11 gliding dead stick with a crew of passengers. Request any pilot to talk them through an engine restart!"

Jeff said to Chuck, "Over to the right at 2 o'clock (*hah, I do know a little flight lingo*), that open strip looks about as good as we'll get."

Chuck knew it wasn't going to be big enough.

"Thanks, Jeff. Strap in."

2000 feet.

Suddenly a new voice came onto the radio, "Flight 11, this is Captain Devlin. My copilot is flippin' through to his restart checklist, but while we're waiting, let's see if ya'll can check some things out for me. Are your engine start levers off?"

Chuck felt an immediate bond with the reassuring mid-Western twang. "Tell him they're off, Jeff."

"'They're off.'"

"All right, good buddy, how 'bout them 'ole engine start switches up top?"

Chuck responded, "They're on."

"They're on."

"Well, all right buddy, how 'bout now ya'll take a look at your fuel flow switches for me?"

Air, spark, fuel, how could I forget something so basic? Now Chuck was mostly mad at himself. "Where are they?"

'Where are they?"

"Just look down right below the engine throttles, good buddy."

Chuck complied and found the fuel flow switches in the "off" position. *Clever bastards!*

"Found 'em!"

"Found 'em!"

"Well, all right, good buddy, my copilot's checklist says ya'll should turn them on next."

Chuck did while glancing out the window at the growing trees. "Done."

"Done."

"Well, all right then, good buddy, let's push one of those engine start levers and see if we can get ya'll goin' up again."

Chuck flipped the left engine to fly.

To his amazement and immense relief, he heard the engine react and begin revving up. He stole another quick glance at the altimeter.

1500 feet.

Jeff shouted into the microphone and the cockpit in general, "'Holy shit, we got one started! Gun it, Chuck!'"

The soothing voice broke back in, "Easy, good buddy, ya'll are probably gonna need to let it spool up for a few seconds. Ya'll also need to push hard on the rudder pedals until we can get that other engine started."

Chuck muttered, "I'm not sure we have a few seconds." But he did start feeling the aircraft pushing to the right and began countering with rudder.

1000 feet.

"Come on, baby, come on!"

Jeff's shouting did not seem as loud to Chuck as his heartbeat as he watched the airspeed indicator begin to creep forward. *Man is this going to be close!* I might be able to pull it off if only I could get a little more speed…

I can! Chuck knew it was a risky option this close to the ground, but decided to take it and quickly reached over and retracted the landing gear.

500 feet.

"Come on, baby, come on!"

With the landing gear up, the airspeed arrow fairly leapt over the orange strip marking what Chuck guessed was the 130 knot minimum takeoff speed of the 767. The engine was pushing harder now.

200 feet.

"I think we're gonna make it, Jeff."

"'Thank Christ!'" Jeff exclaimed as he looked out and saw their descent to the trees holding steady.

90 feet.

Chuck continued using rudder to compensate for the engine. It would be a waste to restart the engine only to auger in because he couldn't control their flight attitude. Finally he felt the plane level off and, after what seemed like another eternity, start to gently rise.

Jeff broke him out of his trance-like state. "'What do you need me to do?'"

100 feet.

Chuck found himself sweating profusely. *But at least we're going up!* "Tell my new favorite pilot that we are at 140 knots and climbing. Ask when we should retract the flaps."

"'Will do, stud! Captain, are you there? We're still in the air! What do we do now?'"

"Nice to hear ya'll are still with us, good buddy. Here's what I need ya'll to do for me now."

0857 – The Pentagon, Arlington, VA

Max Bielke was preparing to begin his 0900 Army Retirement Services meeting when the word came through the corridors that the Pentagon had to be evacuated immediately.

Seriously?! The meeting is supposed to start in less than five minutes. Max wondered what the threat was that would cause an evacuation of the entire building. 40,000 people milling around in the parking lot outside sounded like it was going to be an enormous mosh pit. *At least it is a nice day outside.*

0857:30 – Otis Air Force Base, Massachusetts

Lizard and Chop were cleared to take off from Otis Air National Guard Base in their F-15Cs. Lizard took off first, followed seconds later by Chop.

0858 – Newark International Airport, Newark, New Jersey

Lee Chang saw the latest message come over the Newark airport hotline. *One airplane has been hijacked by Arab men. Search for East Coast departing airlines with four, repeat four, Arab men aboard.* Perfect, right as he was finishing up his search for five Arabs. *I wish those guys would make up their minds.* Back to the drawing board. Were there one or two flights he had found already that had had four Arab men on board? Maybe they want more than just Los Angeles flights now.

0859 – Harrisburg, Pennsylvania

Elliott's mind drifted back to the sports conversation he had with Smith. As he thought about it, he was even surer that Drew Bledsoe had gotten hurt early in that season. But hadn't the NFL changed their schedule after the attack? So what if 9/11 hadn't happened? If the NFL hadn't changed the schedule, maybe the games wouldn't have played out the same way. Maybe Bledsoe doesn't get hurt. Big changes didn't have to come strictly from big shifts. Even little changes could produce big shifts in the future. What was that theory that the stats department people liked to talk about? The Butterfly Effect… where a butterfly flapping its wings could create a hurricane on the other side of the world. It didn't seem so silly to Elliott now. So maybe the Super Bowl advice he had given Detective Smith wasn't worthwhile. Brady is a great player, and probably would have eventually gone on to a great career with New England or another team, but who knows, maybe he would have been traded to Detroit. So Elliott's actions could directly result in a different outcome for people today. But on the other hand, it didn't have to be change for the worse. After all, that was what he was trying to do right now, so he could also have the chance to remake a life for the better. His mind started to drift as he considered the many lives that he could potentially change. It could be a celebrity, or a friend, or coworker or even a close family member…such as…

…such as…damn! Was it possible? With a shudder of emotion he realized he had to see if the opportunity he thought he had was for real.

"I want my phone call."

Smith had been quietly reviewing his notes and was slightly taken aback by the burst of energy from Graham. "What?"

"I want my phone call now."

"Are you going to make another bomb threat?"

"No. I'll make the call right here. You can dial it yourself and listen in, I don't care."

Smith thought to himself, when this guy gets passionate, he doesn't mess around. Silently he pushed the phone across the desk to Elliott.

Elliott felt his fingers trembling as he dialed the familiar number. After a moment the line connected. He heard three rings from the other end, the phone was answered and a female voice came on saying, "Hello?"

The calm, reassuring sound made his heart race even faster. It was her. Just like that.

"Hello? Who is this?"

Elliott mustered the courage to respond "Hello."

"Why, good morning, son. Is everything okay?"

Elliott tried, not very successfully, to stifle a sob as he said to her, "Mom, I sure am glad to hear your voice."

"I'm glad to hear from you too Honey, but you just called us on Sunday. You sound upset, are you sure you're all right?

"Yes, Mom." How long had it been since he had been able to say that?

"Well your voice sure sounds strange. You can't fool your mother you know. What's wrong? Is it something with that girl?"

Elliott was taken aback by the question. "Which one?"

"Honey, you need to get some rest. You remember, the girl you met last month who works in a restaurant."

Oh jeez, Sandy. Elliott didn't think he had been completely dishonest when telling Mom about her. Technically, Hooters is a restaurant. "No Mom. I'm afraid that one isn't going to work out." Not that she hadn't been fun though.

"Well Honey, I sure liked Marlene. Maybe she would like to hear from you again."

"I don't think Marlene is going to work out either."' He was having trouble dredging up his memories from ten years ago to keep up with Mom. Then he had a thought. *Why not?* "I'll tell you what though, I may have a good prospect coming up."

He could feel the surge of interest on the other end of the line. "Do tell."

What the heck, maybe it would work out after all. "Well, she's a nurse. She has brown hair and a smile that takes over the room."

"When did you get interested in brunettes?"

"People can change, Mom." Like a slap in the face, that sentence brought him forcefully back into focus. "Mom, I'm kinda in the middle of something and don't have a lot of time, and I need to talk to you about something. Promise you'll do something for me."

"Anything, honey."

"Look, this is going to sound crazy, and I may never mention it again. In fact, I may even forget that I ever had this conversation with you."

"Honey, do you need to lie down for a while?"

"Mom, please listen to me. If in a couple of years, if you start feeling pain in your stomach, I want you to promise me you'll go straight to the doctor."

Silence. "Honey, why are you scaring me?"

"Promise me you'll do this for me."

"I…I don't understand…"

Elliott practically shouted into the line, "Promise me!"

It was the most excited Detective Smith had seen him get the entire morning.

"Okay, honey, I'll promise to go see a doctor later if you'll promise to go see one now."

Elliott breathed a sigh of relief. "Okay Mom, I'll try to go tomorrow."

"No maybes, honey. You do it for your mother."

"I will, Mom."

After a moment, "That was more drama than I was expecting on a Tuesday morning. Speaking of drama, would you like to talk to your father?"

You don't know the half of how exciting this Tuesday morning might get, "Thanks, I'll catch him another time."

"Okay, honey, don't work too hard today."

Always worried about me more than herself. "Don't worry I won't, Mom."

"I love you, honey."

"I love you too, Mom."

"Bye bye, Elliott."

"Bye, Mom."

Elliott slowly placed the receiver back on the phone and looked up to see Smith locked in the same position he had been in when the conversation started, his bemusement replaced with pained sympathy.

Elliott said, "Dad is a bit of a hypochondriac, so we were caught completely off-guard when Mom got sick. The doctor said that attacking that tumor even a few weeks sooner might have made the difference. She never even got to meet her grandchildren."

He didn't even mention to her that he is sitting in a police station. Smith had lost his closest uncle to cancer and always got a small knot in his stomach whenever he thought of Uncle Dexter. "I am sorry."

"Thanks. Who knows, maybe I just made a difference."

0901 – American Airlines Flight 11

Jeffrey Coombs reported to Boston Center that they were climbing through 2000 feet at 170 knots. He had also gotten on the intercom to ask the medical volunteer to come forward. Then he turned to Chuck. "Okay, so how 'not exactly' a pilot are you?"

"Well, I watched the pilots and we all got to play with the controls in the simulator a little bit. Now I wish I had played with the controls more. If we can find a doctor and get a pilot revived, that would help our chances a lot."

Chuck had just finished talking when a blonde girl carrying the airplane first-aid kit appeared in the cockpit and said, "I'm Carol. I work in a hospital. Who can I help?"

0902 – United Airlines Flight 175

Hamza al-Ghamdi knew something was wrong. He thought that their flight was slowly losing altitude, and now he could see that he was correct. Commercial airliners usually descended at a faster rate. Clearly they were descending slower than usual, thus in all probability, deliberately. They were landing far too early, and the pilots had not mentioned a mechanical problem, so the early landing was most likely due to their team. The only logical reason they would do that was to delay the passengers figuring out that they were landing, in this case specifically him and the other two mujahedeen. Police would almost certainly arrest them when they arrived on the ground. Hamza felt that their chance to strike was ebbing away.

Ahmed al-Ghamdi knew his brother's body language. He sensed, as Hamza also doubtless did, that they were being diverted into landing early. Hamza desperately wanted to carry out their mission. To Ahmed, who was also prepared to be martyred for Allah, the problem was that it *would* be desperate. His earlier assessment of the situation had not changed. They were down to three team members who were on the wrong end of the airplane with an armed security man between them and their objective, the cockpit. Even if they got past him and up to fifty other people, they had to break into the cockpit and disable the pilots before they could land. If the pilots got the plane on the ground, the mission was over. Even if they did get control of the plane in the air, none of them could pilot to their original objective. Ahmed and Hamza had been selected for the team to suppress the passengers and crew only. Ahmed knew that Mohand al-Shehri was also prepared and enthusiastic about carrying out the mission, and could potentially turn it into a partial success. Ahmed had also wanted to carry out a mission, not a back-alley fight. Right now he was trying to talk to Mohand and convince him not to do anything rash. They had still not done anything illegal at the airport or on this flight. Ahmed felt their best chance still lay in patience and cooperation.

0903 – Flight Alpha Kilo

Lizard and Chop had gotten airborne and were vectored on a projected intercept to Flight 11. Lizard was briefed that the hijackers might be using the plane as a flying suicide bomb. He was prepared to do what was needed to protect his country, and had trained to do it his entire adult life. Nonetheless, he was distinctly uneasy over the idea of shooting down a plane full of his fellow Americans. He was sure the same thoughts were going through Chop's mind, but he was keeping them to himself. That was why Lizard liked having Chop on his wing. He epitomized the old fighter pilot joke that the only three things a flight leader ever needed to hear from a good wingman were "Two," "Lead you're on fire," and "I'll take the fat one."

0904 – Charleston International Airport, Charleston, South Carolina

Evan Ames was glancing through the FAA messages that had been coming in that morning, then tried to look casual as he announced that he was going on break and strode out of the airport flight office. He pulled out his cell phone and a lightly dog-eared business card from his wallet, then dialed the number on the card.

A voice responded, "Associated Press."

"Is Paulina Gradowski there?"

"One minute, please." Evan glanced around to make sure no one was nearby.

"This is Paulina."

"My name is Evan. I work at Charleston Airport. You gave me your card last year when you were out here doing the fuel leakage bit."

"I remember the story, but I give my card to a lot of people. How can I help you?"

Evan figured there was no point in being subtle. "How much do you pay your informants?"

"That depends on what they give me." Although she was willing to be more flexible on a slow news day like today.

"There is a big national story shaping up this morning. Are you interested?"

"It better not be more fuel leakage."

Evan knew what he was doing was against their rules, and was sure that years ago he never even would have thought about doing something like this, but his SUV payments and kid's dental bills sure weren't going to go away all by themselves. Besides, if he didn't do it, he told himself that someone else from another airport would, if they weren't already. If the press was going to get the story, at least he would give them the right one.

"How about a plane hijacking, and potentially other hijackings?"

Evan could feel the surge of interest coming through the line and knew the answer before the reporter even said, "Where are you calling from?"

0905 – Boston, Massachusetts

Ed Zwick knew that they had a tough task ahead of them. He also knew how fortunate they were for the guardian angel in the form of Captain Devlin who had kept the airplane in the air and was working with them to get the second engine started. A NASA space engineer as pilot? That was almost good news, probably. The most sensible course seemed to be to bring the aircraft right back to Logan and try to land it there. Ordinarily a problem aircraft would be diverted to an isolated airfield, but in this case, they thought it was important to try to keep the environment as familiar as possible for the nascent crew. As a coast-to-coast flight, it would have plenty of fuel, so they had a lot of time (relatively speaking) to get the spaceman trained to bring the plane down in one piece after they got the second engine restarted. He also had to get a qualified physician on the line to talk to the woman who had stepped up to try and provide medical care to the injured, which apparently included both pilots. *Odd, why would the hijackers disable both pilots? Who were they going to get to fly the plane to their non-extradition nation of choice? Maybe one of them knew how to fly, although that would be uncommon. Hijackers normally just made their pilot hostages fly for them.*

He now had a pilot available to talk to Flight 11 from the ground and reluctantly bid farewell to Captain Devlin, who was preparing to land his own aircraft (although he had offered to remain aloft in order to "give my good buddies a bit of help"). It still seemed surreal to listen to the pilot using the plane's original call sign. "American Airlines Flight 11, now that you're at 10,000 feet, let's get that second engine started, okay?"

Jeffrey Coombs responded, "Okay. Chuck, he wants us to start the second engine."

"Okay. Can you hold us steady, Jeff? You have to kick that rudder fairly hard."

"I got it...kinda."

"Good enough, we have some altitude to play with." Actually, compared to where they had been, 10,000 feet seemed far higher than he ever would have been on the shuttle. "Starting the right engine now." Chuck reached up and moved the engine dial to fly.

Nothing.

Chuck flipped it to off and back again.

Nothing.

Goddammit! "Logan, this is Flight 11, no response from the engine."

The pilot replied, "Okay, check the fuel flow panel."

Chuck looked up. "Looks like normal fuel flow."

"Okay, try activating the cross feed switch and attempt a restart."

"Stand by." Chuck flipped the fuel switch over and re-hacked the engine switch.

Nothing.

"Still a negative on the restart Logan."

"Is your APU on?"

Chuck looked up. "Yep."

"Roger, flip it off and back on and try the engine again."

Chuck complied, then again.

Nothing.

Dammit! "That's a negative Logan."

Ed Zwick's tough task was going to be a lot tougher.

0907 – Dayton, Ohio

Deb was still frowning even after she had hung up the phone and walked out of the kitchen. That had certainly been a strange call from Elliott. Her son was usually level-headed (like herself, she proudly thought) and not given to paranoia or future gloom-and-doom. He called once a week pretty regularly, so she did not expect to hear from him twice in three days. And he never asked her any questions about her health. Usually, he was more worried about his father. In private, they both joked that the man was an incurable hypochondriac, but that didn't mean that they stopped being concerned about him.

Her husband asked her, "Who was that?"

"Elliott."

"Oh. Is something wrong?"

"That's what I asked him. He said no, but I'm not so sure."

"He didn't want to talk to me?" *Like I'm not even here.*

Deb heard the twinge of annoyance in her husband's voice. "No. He sounded really weird though. The whole conversation was very odd."

"Um-hmm."

If her husband was more annoyed than worried, she probably didn't need to be worried either. He always said she worried too much. Every now and then, he was even right. On the bright side, the girl Elliott had mentioned sounded intriguing and seemed to have sunk a hook into him. Like every mom, she just wanted to see her son happy, preferably with some kids that Grandma could spoil. Maybe something would come of this one.

It was an odd call, but not the oddest she had ever gotten from her son. *Oh well, time to return to the day at hand.* "Maybe we can give him a call this evening or tomorrow afternoon. How is your back this morning, dear?"

0908 – United Airlines Flight 175

Ahmed al-Ghamdi gripped Mohand al-Shehri's arm so hard his knuckles were turning white, but Mohand still seemed determined to start an attack. The security man who had come on board the airplane before takeoff was now openly watching them as Ahmed tried to restrain Mohand and calm Hamza. It was true that Mohand could perform some piloting of the aircraft, but not if he was dead, and it seemed unlikely that the first person to rush the armed security man would come away uninjured. Ahmed felt his heart racing, but he kept telling himself that he was only trying to stop this mission because it was not a good mission, not because he was afraid.

0911 – Flight Alpha Kilo

The F-15's KY-58 crackled. "Alpha Kilo 1, this is Ops."

"Go ahead, Ops."

"That hijacked plane is back under passenger control."

Lizard had not expected that. "They're sure? They want us to go check? We'll be there in like four minutes."

"I understand, Alpha Kilo 1, but they said no. There are reports that there could be other planes to be hijacked, so we need to keep a presence in the air. It's going to take us a little while to get another flight airborne. You may have to shoot down the next hijacked track, understood?"

Lizard thought, *No kidding. If I have a problem with that, I'm probably the wrong person to be sitting in a single seat fighter. What's the matter with these guys?* Oh well, there was no point in being unprofessional on the air.

"Copy Ops."

"Direct that you proceed to New York and take station in Whiskey 105 off Long Island."

"Copy, Ops. Chop?"

"Two copies."

"'Sounds like this may just end up being a milk run, Chop. Still beats sitting in the Ready Room. Turn to heading 090, climb to 25,000 feet and then slow to 400 knots."

"Two."

0912 – United Airlines Flight 175

Jeremy Blivens had lost patience for keeping up the charade that he was an ordinary passenger. He figured they would be on the ground in about fifteen or twenty minutes. The suspects had probably figured that out as well, so if they were going to act, they probably knew they would have to make up their mind to do it before it was too late. Jeremy decided this was a good time to preempt them. He could take the heat for it after he got back home alive. Office politics suddenly seemed a lot less important to Jeremy than living through the day. He made eye contact with the flight attendant and nodded his head, got out of his seat and moved over to the lady in seat 28C.

Jeremy never took his eyes off his suspects as he said, "Ma'am, I am a Federal Air Marshal. We have a potential security situation on board the aircraft. Would you please calmly but quickly move forward to an empty seat?"

Deborah Medwig was only too happy to comply. The forty-six-year-old redhead always insisted that she and her husband travel on separate airplanes because she didn't want their daughter to become an orphan on a single day. She had suspected that the three suspicious-looking young men were being placed in the back for a reason, and not a good one. She had been too afraid to move earlier, but now she was only too happy to comply with the marshal's direction.

"Certainly, sir, I'll move right now. May I get my bag first?"

"Why don't you wait until after we land, ma'am. Okay?"

"Maybe I'll go look for a seat in first class," Deborah said as she got up and began moving forward.

Jeremy smiled thinly as he said softly after her, "Good idea, ma'am. I know there are three empties up there." With that minor problem settled, Jeremy turned his full attention back to the suspects and moved slowly but decisively back to the aisle that was now an unobstructed path between him and his three suspects.

"Gentlemen, for your own safety, I am going to ask you one at a time to come out from your seats, lie face down in the aisle, and allow me to secure your wrists with flex cuffs." As he spoke, he drew his pistol and pointed it down at the aisle in the direction of the suspects so that he was not targeting any specific one.

Three hostile faces glared back at him.

I was afraid of this. Jeremy committed himself to action, "Gentlemen, for your own safety, I must ask you one at a time to come out of your seats and lie face down in the aisle to allow me to secure you for the remainder of the flight."

Hamza shouted back at him, "No one provides for my safety but Allah!"

Ahmed's voice in Arabic came from behind him, "Brother, calm yourself, today is not the day, Allah wills it."

0913 – American Airlines Flight 11

Whatever was wrong with the right engine on their troubled airplane, they apparently weren't going to be able to fix it before it returned to earth. Ed Zwick and the pilot had trouble-shot every combination of electronics and fuel without being able to restart the right engine. Both men in the cockpit had searched every square inch looking for a pulled panel or ripped wiring, to no avail. The left engine seemed to be working steadily enough, but Ed was not enthusiastic about letting the passengers attempt the difficult task of learning how to fly while circling in the pattern of a major airport at low altitude on one engine.

"Flight 11, that engine just doesn't feel like starting for us. I'm afraid we're going to have to give up on the second engine and just focus on trying to get you down with what we have."

Chuck was frustrated as well as skeptical. "That just doesn't make any sense. Maybe the hijackers did something we haven't found yet. Airplane equipment is ordinarily designed to be like 99.99 percent reliable."

"I agree Flight 11, but it looks like today is not going to be ordinary. Let's just keep working on what we can do."

"Roger."

Meanwhile, Logan International Airport was scrambling to clear out aircraft and ready response personnel.

0914 – United Airlines Flight 175

Mohand al-Shehri had had enough of the insolent infidels onboard their airplane (he already thought of it as such). As a youngster, he had an opportunity to study at the Islamic University in Abha, but as his commitment to Wahhabism grew, he neglected his studies until he eventually failed his final examination. He briefly supported the Jihad in Chechnya before deciding to help strike at the heart of Christianity. He applied for a U.S. visa, which was granted to him by the Americans without an interview. He knew that his heart was pure, thus Allah would provide a way for him to succeed. They were so close that it was clearly His will that they go on.

"Yes, Officer, I get down now," Mohand said as he moved out of the seat and towards the air marshal.

0914:30

Jeremy Blivens released the safety as he took a step back, pointed his pistol directly at 31F who was moving toward him, and sternly said, "Sir, get down now or I'll shoot."

Ahmed shouted in Arabic, "No, Mohand, don't do it!"

Mohand coiled and lunged toward the air marshal as he shouted "Allah Akbar."

If there were only one potential hostile, Jeremy might have been willing to stall another half a second. If there weren't passengers right behind him, Jeremy could have continued to retreat. If the suspects hadn't begun shouting in a foreign language, Jeremy might have been willing to give them the benefit of the doubt. With no good options left, Jeremy fired a single shot from his pistol, the bullet lodging in Mohand's left shoulder, shattering the socket around it. Mohand cried as he lurched forward, falling into the agent and knocking him into the aisle. As Mohand fell on top of him, the pistol went off a second time, with the bullet passing in and out of Mohand's stomach.

Jeremy heard the screams from the passengers behind him as he struggled to push the attacker off of him, but he knew that he was now helpless and totally vulnerable to any follow on attack by the remaining suspects.

Hamza al-Ghamdi wished that he had been seated next to Mohand so they could work out an attack plan together. His brother Ahmed was obviously having second thoughts about their mission. Hamza's spirit was in complete accord with Mohand that today was their day to do something, anything, to the infidels. After the security agent had begun confronting them, he had seen Mohand begin to move forward and knew that he was going to keep going. He started to rise up to help Mohand, but was grabbed from behind and pulled back into the seat. He tried to twist free as he shouted in Arabic at his brother "Dammit Ahmed, no!"

"He will kill you for nothing, brother!"

"Let me go, Ahmed!"

"Not today, brother!"

"I go!" Hamza shouted as he finally tore free from his brother's grip and lurched unsteadily into the aisle.

Jeremy Blivens was still trying to free up his pistol arm, surprised that the next attacker was not already on top of him. Now he saw the man from seat 30G coming towards him, but just as the attacker was about to reach Jeremy, he seemed to fall again.

"Stop, Hamza, stop!" shouted Ahmed after he had grabbed his brother's ankle and brought him down in the aisle.

Hamza again wrenched partly loose from Ahmed and rose up on his hands and knees just as Jeremy Blivens succeeded in freeing his pistol hand and began firing the weapon wildly down the aisle. His second shot grazed Hamza's thigh and then went through Ahmed's forehead, entering his brain cavity and instantly killing him.

Hamza's sibling instinct kicked in as he felt the hand gripping his ankle go limp. He knew immediately that his brother had been killed. He looked back at Ahmed in pain and anguish just as Jeremy's final shot took off his own left ear. He knew that their mission was going to fail. His other two team members were dead, and he could see passengers and crew running toward them, appearing to be shouting and brandishing anything they could grab to use as weapons. Hamza was not scared of being martyred in the name of a great cause, but the sights and sound of the losing battle, particularly the shock of his dead brother's lifeless eyes staring back at him from the aisle, suddenly drained him of his energy and will. He sighed greatly and then collapsed face-first onto the floor of the airplane in tears. "Forgive us, Allah, we have failed you."

That was strange, Jeremy thought. 30G was the suspect he had expected to be most likely to start trouble. Jeremy had been caught slightly off-guard when 31F turned out to be the one that started the attack. Jeremy had emptied his revolver when he saw 30G coming at him, but knew he had not put him down and expected 30G to attack him with 31F still on top of him. He was surprised to instead see 30G apparently give up and sag down to the aisle in tears. He dimly heard voices behind him because he had been temporarily deafened by the discharges of his own weapon.

"Get them!"

"Stop them!"

"Don't let them get to the cockpit!"

Jeremy recovered his senses and his voice returned. "Don't kill them, we want them alive! Help me get out from under this damned body now!"

Mark Bavis had come running up to Jeremy. The thirty-one-year-old was a second-year scout for the Los Angeles Kings professional hockey team, after playing at Boston University and coaching at Harvard. He had been annoyed that he was in economy while his boss, Garnet "Ace" Bailey, got to sit in first class, but now he was glad that his seat put him close to the action. When the shooting started, he had decided to do what he could to keep these assholes from taking over the airplane. As he got up he heard his seatmate say, "I'm with you!"

Joe Lopez lived in California and was returning from Boston where he had been temporarily working as a pipe layer. When he saw the man next to him take off for the back, he didn't hesitate to follow him toward the action.

They came up and saw that the air marshal was trying to work his way out from underneath one of the attackers. Mark heard his direction to spare the hijackers, dropped the food tray he had ripped out to use as a weapon, and instead stopped to help the air marshal. Joe quickly followed suit and jumped to the other side of the prone figures.

Jeremy finally felt the hands appear and help pull 31F off of him.

"Officer, you already killed two of them, there's only one left," Joe quietly told the air marshal as he finished pulling the dying hijacker aside.

Jeremy still couldn't hear what the helping passengers were saying, but he finally managed to get up and put a fresh speed load into his pistol. As he did he glanced behind the sobbing assailant. The last guy was definitely dead. Jeremy must have hit him with a stray round while he was firing at 30G. He pulled a zip tie out of his pocket and handed it to one of the passengers who had helped him get free.

"Put this on him, please."

Mark Bavis was only too happy to comply, even though he had never attempted to apply restraints to anyone in his life.

Jeremy turned to the prone attacker. "We're going to secure your hands now. Lie very still. If you so much as twitch a muscle," he placed the barrel right on the back of 30G's head for emphasis, "I will put a hole in your head the size of a plum."

Hamza stared dully back at the agent without comprehending.

Mark didn't know how tight to tie the zip. *Better safe than sorry,* he thought as he cinched it with all his strength.

Jeremy saw 30G wince and felt that he was now in control of the hijackers. He turned around to the flight attendant and asked, "How long until we land?"

"I'll check, sir," Robert Fangman responded.

"The sooner the better. And tell the pilots to call ahead to the airfield. Tell them that the situation onboard is under control, that we have two dead hijackers, one live prisoner in custody, no friendly casualties, and to make sure that there are FBI agents waiting on the ground for us."

Robert Fangman felt a wave of relief come over him as he said, "Yes, sir."

0917 – Charleston, South Carolina

Paulina Gradowski got her second source through a friend who worked in FAA administration and emailed the story release request to her editor at the same time as she dialed the release desk.

"Sandy, this is Paulina. I've got a big story I just emailed to you guys."

"It's coming through now…I got it…wow, okay, that is news! You confirmed this?"

"Of course."

"Right, I'll get the boss' okay and get it out. Will you have a follow-up?"

"I'm working on it." *This might get me off beat work.*

0918 – American Airlines Flight 11

Carol Bouchard had taken stock of the medical situation on board the airplane and was dealing with it as best she could. She was an emergency services secretary at Kent County Hospital emergency room in Warwick, Rhode Island. That meant she was around emergency room activity, knew the terminology, and could take patient readings, but did not participate in actual surgical procedures. She was not comfortable with being designated the flight medic, but she also understood that she was their best option. The tranquilizers she had taken prior to takeoff to calm her for the flight were not helping her stay alert. She had been reluctant to go on this trip due to her fear of flying, but she had been persuaded that the trip would be good for her (she knew they meant well, but at this point she was ready to walk home from wherever they landed).

There were five unconscious hijackers, probably dead or dying, whom she couldn't care less about. The remaining passengers were hauling them to a seat row and stacking them in like firewood with guards posted just in case. There was one dead passenger. Edmund Glazer, who had been sitting next to him, described how the man in 9B had somehow known what was going to happen, borrowed a small knife from him before they even took off, and had whirled and begun stabbing hijackers almost immediately, killing the one who died in the initial takeover and injuring two others. Glazer was adamant that without the heroic actions of 9B, their odds of retaking the aircraft would have been far worse, if not impossible.

On to the living. The older gentleman who had started the counterattack, David, had a broken hand and a slash wound and was in pain, but seemed to be in pretty good spirits. His wife, Lynn, was taking care of him and told Carol that he worked in television (she thought he looked vaguely familiar). A couple of other passengers had some serious cuts and bruises that they had received during the counterattack, both severe cuts from the hijackers and trauma from being thrown around the plane. She thought they needed immediate attention, but everyone was telling her to go the cockpit and tend to the people trying to fly the plane. Without them, it wouldn't matter what she did for anyone else. She treated the injuries to Jeff Coombs, who seemed to be okay. Chuck told her that the most important thing she had to do was try to revive one of the pilots. Apparently, being an astronaut doesn't mean you know everything about flying. She had looked at the younger pilot, whom the crewmembers said was named Thomas, and thought she had stabilized him, but he had been badly injured by blunt force blows to the head and was unresponsive to her. Jeff told her that the older pilot, John, had apparently fought with the hijacker for control of the plane before lapsing back into unconsciousness. He sounded like the best candidate for revival, so she turned her primary attention to him. But she knew she needed to get help for the other injured people before too much longer.

0923 – Harrisburg, Pennsylvania

"I understand, thanks." Detective Smith hung up the phone and turned to Elliott Graham. "Three of the guys from United Flight 175 were allowed to board and tried to take over the plane. Two of them are dead. The other is under control. The plane is diverting into Pittsburgh."

"So they failed?" Elliott was annoyed that anyone had had to die at all, if these people had just listened to him in the first place.

"Yes, they did."

Elliott still felt his exuberance being tempered by caution. "Did they hurt anyone?"

"No reports of casualties other than the hijackers, and I get the feeling we aren't going to miss any of those guys."

Elliott rarely indulged in divine praise, but this seemed like a good time for it. "Thank God."

Smith was in total agreement with Graham. "Thanks, indeed."

0924 – Boston, Massachusetts

Ed Zwick heard the radio crackle to life, "Hey Ed, this is Jeff."

"Go ahead, Jeff. How is everything up there?"

"Okay for the moment, although Carol said that we have some medical problems. Listen, we wanted to pass along a thought to you. When I first got in the cockpit, the hijacker was flying the plane by himself. They had already knocked out both pilots. Chuck says that if this guy knew how to shut down the engines too, then he knew an awful lot about flying a 767 for a random hijacker. We don't know if it means anything, it just seems odd."

"I've been thinking about that myself Jeff, and I agree with you guys. I'll pass your insights along to the feds. There is a report out that there might be other hijacking attempts. In the meantime, I'll be turning you over to Logan Tower shortly. They are supposed to have a pilot and doctor waiting in there to figure out how to bring you down."

"Really? We're not the only ones?"

"Apparently not."

That was a little irritating. If the plot was this big, how had the authorities not noticed it? "What the hell? Who ran the fire sale on terrorists? We do appreciate your help though, Ed."

"Let's just figure out how to bring you in Flight 11."

0925 – United Airlines Flight 93

Captain Jason Stahl and First Officer LeRoy Homer looked at the message that had come across:

Warning: Terrorists have attempted to seize two U.S. flights. Secure cockpits immediately.

Homer asked his captain, "Have you ever seen anything like this Jason?"

"No, I haven't. This is peculiar. Please see if you can contact someone down there and confirm this."

"Roger, sir."

0926 – Harrisburg, Pennsylvania

Detective Smith tried to make sense of everything he had seen that morning. Elliott Graham was relentlessly single-minded in his pursuit of whatever he felt to be true. He certainly was making decisions with no concern for the long-term impact they might have on him. He had probably already lost his job and girlfriend (wife?), and hadn't even thought twice about using his phone call doing something to help someone else, albeit his mother. He hadn't even told her he was in a police station and might need a lawyer. Smith was at a loss as to what to do with him at this point. Obviously charging him with making false threats was out the window. He had cooperated fully and willingly throughout the investigation, so no obstruction of justice option was available either. The only thing left that even conceivably made sense was conspiracy, but what did this guy have in common with a bunch of Middle Eastern hijackers, other than knowing what they were planning to do today? Smith shuddered to think of what might have happened across the country had these guys been able to carry out their plans without interference. They were certainly fanatical. Even with an alerted crew and without their weapons, the first team had briefly succeeded in taking over their aircraft. The second team, at partial strength and also without weapons, had still attempted to hijack its plane until they were all dead or disabled. Imagine the carnage four airplanes full of these guys could have caused if they were in fact suicides. Smith saw the city chief of police had arrived and was motioning to him. He had no idea what he was going to recommend to the boss.

0927 – United Airlines Flight 93

Ziad Jarrah nodded to his three team members who rose to their feet and moved swiftly to their assigned places around the aircraft. Saeed al-Ghamdi moved forward to secure the cockpit while the Ahmads cut off each aisle toward the cockpit. This would be the crucial phase of the operation, where the lack of the fifth hijacker would be most glaring. They were gambling by not using at least two mujahadeen to secure the cockpit, and there would only be a single person left to guard each aisle. If the passengers tried to retake the aircraft, there would be only a single team member in each row, whom the passengers could possibly swarm and overwhelm just by using sheer numbers. Jarrah had decided not to reveal himself until after the aircraft was secured, thereby confusing the passengers and crew and providing a reserve in case the Ahmads were in fact rushed by the passengers. Their hope lay in the normal compliance of westerners when faced with a hijacking, their hope which was in fact the vital assumption underpinning the whole operation.

0928

Flight attendant Debbie Welsh was preparing to begin the in-flight services when she was surprised by the passenger from 1B, who strode right past her toward the cockpit.

Captain Jason Dahl turned as he saw the man break into the cockpit and move towards First Officer LeRoy Homer brandishing some sort of knife. Homer shifted around in the confined space to confront him and the two men began wrestling. Dahl immediately began shouting into the radio "Mayday! Mayday! Mayday!"

A voice responded, "Somebody call Cleveland?"

The Ahmads began screaming at the passengers and crew in the passenger section while waving their knives. Jarrah was grateful to see the stunned, frightened passengers begin moving toward the rear of the aircraft. *Sheep.*

The cockpit intruder had subdued Homer and now moved toward Captain Dahl, who also saw Debbie Welsh moving up behind the intruder. Dahl screamed into the radio and at the assailants, "Mayday! Get out of here! Get out of here."

Saeed al-Ghamdi cut the senior pilot as well, although he was supposed to try to keep one of the pilots conscious to assist Jarrah. He also heard a woman yelling directly behind him, but focused on the man in the seat as the plane began to nose forward.

Ziad Jarrah felt the tilt of the plane and, glancing behind him to see that he was out of view of the passengers and crew, moved toward the cockpit holding his knife. As he entered, he saw Saeed had disabled the pilot on the right and was struggling with the senior pilot, as well as one of the flight attendants.

Captain Dahl had initially been trying to dive the aircraft to throw the attacker off his balance, but saw that LeRoy was unconscious and thought that he was now the only person who could fly the plane. Afraid that the attacker would pummel him into unconsciousness as well, he used the diversion caused by Debbie to set the autopilot and reroute the communications link so that the intercom was transmitting directly to air traffic control.

Zaid Jarrah stabbed Debbie Welsh from behind, then checked to see that Saeed could handle both the attendant and the senior pilot. Satisfied, he moved to the right side, pulled the limp form of the co-pilot from the seat, and moved into his place. As the aircraft had already regained altitude control, he turned on what he thought was the intercom and said "Ladies and gentlemen, this is the captain. Please sit down and keep remaining seated. We have a bomb on board. So sit."

To his surprise, a voice responded saying "Calling Cleveland Center unreadable. Say again, slowly." Before he could recover, he was attacked from behind by the accursed flight attendant and turned to deal with her once and for all. With Saeed's help, they were finally able to subdue the troublesome woman. That left only the senior pilot among the crew in the cockpit still conscious, lying on the cockpit floor moaning.

Saeed looked down at her unmoving figure, then back up at Jarrah and said "Everything fine. I finished." Jarrah nodded and Saeed exited the cockpit to help the Ahmads (Jarrah's inside joke) keep the passengers under control. Then Jarrah took over the autopilot and instructed it to turn east and climb to 40,000 feet.

0930 – Pittsburgh International Airport, Pittsburgh, Pennsylvania

As United Flight 175 touched down at the airport in Pittsburgh, passenger Touri Bolourchi was staring at the bound hijacker as well as the two who had been killed. Touri was a retired nurse who had fled from Iran in 1979 after the Islamic Revolution when Ayatollah Khomeini had ordered the schools closed. She was determined to ensure her daughters were educated and brought them with her to California where they were all later joined by her husband. Being forced to leave the country of her birth had given her a particular distaste for religious extremism. She considered herself a devout Muslim and said her daily prayers, but she mixed her belief with an enjoyment of life that included a zest for cooking and reading. She did not force her religious views on her own daughters, and certainly would not have done it to someone else. She did not care for the unsmiling, unfeeling zealots of any religious affiliation who had convinced themselves that their god wanted them to oppress and kill other human beings in Her name. As she looked at the three assailants who could shout "Allah

Akbar" as they attempted to terrorize people who had done them no harm, she flashed back to the same thought she had had while watching things come apart in Tehran, *How can these people be reading the same Koran as me?*

0932 – American Airlines Flight 11

Carol Bouchard had returned to the cabin and confirmed her worst fears. The other two passengers were in critical condition. Both were clammy and unresponsive to her. The trauma and loss of blood they had endured needed immediate treatment by qualified physicians. She had also looked at one of the older passengers who was exhibiting heart attack symptoms, including chest pain and shortness of breath. She went back to tell the flyers that the medical situation in the cabin was getting critical and beyond her ability to cope with. Landing soon and getting them to qualified medical experts was their best hope.

0934

Jeffrey Coombs was talking to the doctor dialed into the communication channel. The doctor agreed with Carol; the passengers' medical situation was becoming serious, and a sustained period of time on the airplane was going to become dangerous to them.

0935 – Cleveland, Ohio

Air Traffic Control saw United Flight 93 radically change direction and altitude and began scrambling to move aircraft out of their flight path. They also notified the FAA that they had a potential hijacking in their sector.

0936 – United Airlines Flight 93

Todd Beamer was trying to figure out what to do. He knew that the consensus opinion of what to do in the event of a hijacking was to obey the assailants and not try to fight back. But his antennae were up, and this situation did not seem right to him. The first-class passengers and flight crew were whispering that the Arabs had severely assaulted the pilots. That didn't make sense; the hijackers would need the pilots to get them where they wanted to go. How many terrorists know how to fly a 757 jumbo jet? And the East Coast of the U.S. seemed about as far away from safe destinations for terrorists as it was possible to get. Who around here did they think was going to welcome them in, the Canadians? He and other passengers were trying to surreptitiously make phone calls to family and friends. Maybe they could get some information from the outside. His own attempt to make a credit card call on the airplane phone to his wife was routed through customer service to a GTE supervisor to whom he was now relaying details of the hijacking.

0937 – Atlanta, Georgia

Copy associate Pascal Gilmont at CNN was monitoring the copy wire when he saw the latest AP release.

American Airlines Flight 11 out of Boston has been hijacked by five Arab men armed with knives. Inside sources indicate this hijacking may be part of a larger conspiracy to hijack a number of passenger airplanes in the continental United States.

Pascal turned immediately, picked up his phone, and called his boss.

"I'm sending you an AP release, Chief. It's hot."

0938 – Flight Alpha Kilo

"Alpha Kilo 1, Ops."

Lizard keyed the microphone. "Go, Ops."

"Got another possible one. United Flight 93 out of Newark."

"Where is it going?"

"Right now it is vectored east from around Pittsburgh. We're not sure where it's going. Request you turn heading 240 to Philly immediately."

"Copy that, Ops. Chop?"

"Two."

0939 – United Airlines Flight 93

Saeed came into the aircraft cockpit, still out of breath and coming down from the adrenaline rush, and told Jarrah that although the passengers were in the back of the aircraft, they were still acting unruly and making phone calls. Jarrah nodded, activated the intercom, and said "Uh, this is the captain. I would like you all to remain seated. There is a bomb on board and we're going back to the airport, and to have our demands met. Please remain quiet." As he clicked off, he remembered that his previous intercom call had received a response from a ground controller. The pilot must have changed the intercom setting so that he had been broadcasting outside the aircraft without knowing it. Looking over, he found the communication switch and toggled it back to its normal setting. Jarrah did not consider it to be more than a minor setback.

0940 – Cleveland, Ohio

Cleveland control heard this latest transmission. They had already concluded that the speaker did not realize he was broadcasting outside the aircraft. In conjunction with American Airlines Flight 11's takeover and the attempt on United Flight 175, it was clear that this was another part of a conspiracy of aircraft seizures ongoing in the U.S. Cleveland relayed the latest transmission to the FAA's main office.

0940:30 – United Airlines Flight 93

Thomas Burnett was one of the passengers being moved to the back of the aircraft by the hijackers. As he blended into the group of frightened people, he picked up one of the GTE air phones and called his wife at their home on San Ramon, California. He had been a football quarterback all the way up through college at Saint John's University, Minnesota, until an injury ended his playing days. He went on to earn degrees in Business Management, and had risen to become senior vice-president and COO of a medical devices company. For nearly a year he had been going to church on a daily basis, trying to address a sense of foreboding that he was feeling. *Boy do I hate being right,* he thought to himself.

"Hello?"

He felt a rush of relief to hear her voice. "Honey, its Tom. My plane has been hijacked and we have been herded to the back of the plane. There are three hijackers. They've stabbed one person and another claims he has a bomb."

His wife was shocked, but she had also been a flight attendant before getting married and felt she knew what to do. "Tom, please find someplace to sit quietly and not draw attention to yourself."

"I'll try. I have to get off this line. Find out what you can and I'll try to call you back in a few minutes. I love you."

0941 – Boston, Massachusetts

Fifty-five-year-old Marty Jackson was WBZ Radio's traffic helicopter reporter. He loved his job and was a well-known voice over Greater Boston as he helped the citizens navigate their daily commute. However, at the moment, he was interested in the FAA guidance to all aerial traffic in Boston to clear out a heading directly leading to Logan's runway. He had been in the air long enough that he recognized the controllers clearing a path for an emergency landing. He was still supposed to be covering his daily beat, but his instincts told him that this might turn out to be a much better story than the end of rush hour traffic.

"Tower, this is WBZ traffic."

"Hey Marty, you stuck in traffic again?"

"That joke never gets old guys. Something's going on. I'm pretty sure they just cleared out an emergency heading to Logan. Can you check and find out what's going on?"

"We'll get back to you, Marty. Do you have fuel left to stay up?"

"Enough for a while. I'm going to go get as close to the flight path as I can. Get ready to capture a live video feed."

"Okay, Marty. Happy hunting."

0942 – Harrisburg, Pennsylvania

Detective Smith was in the conference room when Officer Jenny Parrish knocked on the door and, without waiting, rushed in to breathlessly exclaim, "Another plane was hijacked!"

Detective Smith nodded thanks and then turned back to his boss. "I need to get back to Mr. Graham, sir."

"Go ahead. I guess I need to call the mayor. I don't know

what I'm going to do, but figure out a way to keep this guy here."

"Yessir, but I don't think that that is going to be a problem. And please try and keep the FBI out of here. I would rather wait as long as I can before bringing them in, and I don't think they will have a good effect on the source." As Smith continued back to the interrogation room he knew that in his own mind, Graham was no longer a criminal suspect. He also knew they wouldn't be able to drag Graham away before this was over.

0943

Graham looked up and saw Smith return to the room. "Another plane was hijacked.'"

Elliott quickly felt livid again and exploded, "God dammit, Detective, is everyone just sitting around with their thumbs up their asses?"

Smith was disappointed as well, but maintained his professionalism. "We've got a lot of people trying to fit a lot of pieces together in a hurry, Mr. Graham."

"Which flight?"

"United Flight 93 out of Newark."

Elliott thought intently. He was pretty sure that was the plane whose passengers had attempted to retake the aircraft from the terrorists and crashed into the Pennsylvania field. The "Let's Roll" guy would have been one of the passengers. Any of the details he could remember about their story would probably help. Now he wished he had seen the movie.

Detective Smith was no longer cavalier about interrupting Graham's train of thought and instead watched him intently.

Graham finally looked back at Smith and spoke. "There was one plane that fought back. The passengers overran the cockpit and the hijacker pilot apparently crashed the plane into the ground rather than let them retake the aircraft."

"Is it this one?"

"There is a good chance it is."

"Why did they fight back and not the others?"

"Their plane was hijacked last, which appears to be the case *again* today. The passengers and crew were herded into the back and they used their cell phones to communicate with friends and family on the outside and learned about the other suicide crashes after they had happened. We'll never know for sure, but they must have figured out that they were going to crash too, so they decided to take their chances attempting to recover the plane from the terrorists."

"Do you have any idea where the plane was going?"

"Again, I don't know, but the best evidence we had indicates that they were probably heading for the White House or Capitol Hill."

"So it's going to DC?"

"Yep."

"I'll put out a notice. Do you specifically know the names of any of the passengers or crewmembers who fought back?"

"There was one guy in particular. The last thing his wife heard during her phone call with him was him saying "Let's roll" to the other passengers on the plane. I could probably remember his name if I saw the passenger list."

"You got it. Jenny, call the FBI liaison immediately and recommend they evacuate the White House and Capitol Hill." *Even though they'll probably get even more interested in our suspect.*

Elliott Graham looked over at him and blandly said, "The president isn't there."

"Excuse me?" *Now what?*

"The president isn't at the White House. He isn't in DC this morning. He's visiting a school in Florida right now."

"How do you know?"

"We all know. The press was filming him as he was reading to some elementary school kids when an aide came into the classroom and whispered the news of the attacks to him. We've all seen the clip about thirty times. Give him credit, he didn't flinch."

"Thanks for the info, but they still need to evacuate the buildings in DC." *Amazing.*

0944 – American Airlines Flight 11

Chip Hansen had just retaken control of Flight 11 as it reentered Boston's airspace. He had been brought up to speed on the situation. They had passengers trying to fly a 767 with one engine out. They had tried continually to restart the engine with no success. They also had a number of badly injured passengers on the plane. The plane had plenty of fuel, so in theory they weren't in a rush to land. But the engine problem and the medical issues meant that the situation on board could get worse at any time. The man flying the plane, Chuck Jones, was actually exhibiting a high degree of confidence, all things considered.

On behalf of Chuck, Jeffrey Coombs said, "He thinks we need to put down as soon as we can."

"Understood, Flight 11, but right now you have about an hour of flying experience. Landing with an engine out is tough for a veteran pilot. We would like to give you some more practice time before you try to land."

"Yep, but we've got hurt people up here getting worse, and Chuck doesn't trust the engines on this thing. He figures the hurt people are going to get worse faster than he can get better at flying, so let's take our best shot right now."

"Okay, Flight 11, it's your call. Turn to heading 085 and start a descent to 2500 feet. Good luck, Flight 11."

Jeffrey Coombs responded, "Got it. Thanks, man."

0945 – Air Traffic Control System Command Center, Herndon, Virginia

FAA National Operations Office was busy dealing with an unprecedented crisis. On a normal day, they were responsible for controlling over 4,000 daily commercial flights in the United States.

They now had the latest report confirming that a second attempted hijacking had occurred over the continental U.S. in addition to the attempted takeover of UA Flight 175 that had resulted in the deaths of two of the hijackers. Combined with the aircraft boarding denial that had occurred in DC with American Airlines Flight 77, it was clear that there was a large conspiracy underway utilizing the air transportation system in the United States. The FAA did not know what their objective was, and at this point had no idea how many more potential hijacking teams had not revealed themselves. It was probable that the hostiles would have had all their attacks occur nearly simultaneously, expecting that the U.S. would react by shutting down opportunities for follow-on attacks. In that case, all of the hijackings might already be in progress. A total of four events would also dovetail with the FBI tip that had been put out earlier. But the FAA leadership couldn't be sure, and airplanes loaded with passengers and fuel were risky dice to gamble with. No one had ever simultaneously grounded every aircraft in the United States before, but then no one had ever faced a situation like this. They felt the situation was too risky to need to wait for a decision to be made by someone higher in the bureaucracy. On their own authority, they made the decision to ground all civilian aircraft in the United States immediately.

0947 – Harrisburg, Pennsylvania

Jenny Parrish knocked and came into the office where Elliott and Detective Smith were still chatting quietly.

"Detective, the press has the story. It's on AP."

"That was just a matter of time. What does the release say?"

Jenny read from the computer printout she had been handed before coming into the office. "American Airlines Flight 11 out of Boston has been hijacked by five Arab men armed with knives. Inside sources indicate this hijacking may be part of a larger conspiracy to hijack passenger airplanes in the continental United States."

Elliott Graham was surprised. "How did they get the story so quickly?"

"It's what reporters do, and they pay people a lot of money to get their information. We always fight the media time crunch. It's not all bad news. Maybe it will help us get the word to the passengers and crew on Flight 93." Smith was more worried that they were going to track the story to the police station and swarm the facility, a distraction he didn't need.

Elliott was not very optimistic.

"It may, but since none of these teams have carried out a successful mission yet, it still isn't going to help the people on Flight 93 understand that the guys who control their airplane are suicides, not regular hijackers."

"I understand, still, let's hope for the best." *Work with me here man...* Then across the room, "Jenny, please check on that flight manifest for me again."

"Yessir."

0948 – United Airlines Flight 93

Todd Beamer was still describing the situation on board the aircraft to the GTE supervisor he had been initially routed to. There were two hijackers controlling the crowd, one with a knife and one with a bomb strapped to his waist. Curiously, the hijackers were not making much of an attempt to prevent the passengers and crew from making phone calls, even out-of-sight aircrew members. Perhaps they felt threatened as there were only two of them guarding the hostages, but it seemed like a cavalier attitude to take towards passengers and crewmembers who could be providing information to potential rescue teams.

0949 – Harrisburg, Pennsylvania

Detective Smith had enough things to do, but he had remembered that he could check out another piece of Graham's story. He flipped through his Rolodex to find a number he hadn't called in a while and dialed.

The operator on the other end said, "Penn State campus police."

"Marty Gossler, please."

"Certainly. May I tell him who's calling, please?"

"Bill Smith."

"Thank you. One moment, please."

The familiar voice came onto the other end of the line. "Bill, I haven't heard from you in a while. How the hell are you?"

Smith was glad to hear his old partner's voice again. "Pretty good, Marty. How is Ellen?"

"Doing all right. She'll be glad to hear you asked about her. How is my old stomping ground? You haven't let it go completely to hell have you?"

"Harrisburg is Harrisburg, you know how it goes."

"I do have days when I miss it down there, but we're still glad we came up here when the kids started going to school. So what can I do for you? Have you heard about all the stuff that's going on in the air today?"

The word was getting around. "Funny, that's why I called you. Do you have a minute?"

"Sure, but I don't know how I can help."

Smith knew exactly how he wanted to set up their conversation to steer it in the right direction. "Well, I've got a guy in the office who claimed to have foreknowledge of these events because he's from the future."

"Oh, that's great stuff. I love the weirdos. Did I ever tell you about the seventy-year-old nudist who said she had been Charlemagne's masseuse?"

"About a hundred times. Anyway, this guy told me a bunch of goofy stuff based on his ability to move through time."

"Like what?"

"Well, one of them was right up your alley, so I wanted to share it with you."

"Do tell."

"He came out with this story that there is a football coach right there at the college who is molesting little boys on campus. Then he claims that the university knows that it's going on and isn't doing anything about it."

Marty had stopped laughing. The long silence told Detective

Smith everything he needed to know. *Holy shit!*

"Marty?"

"Who is this source of yours?"

"It's not important. What are you not telling me, Marty?"

Another long silence. "Bill, this is a great program that is important to everyone in this city, hell, in the whole damn state. Folks around here are proud of their football team and would not take kindly to a lot of wild stories about the school coming out. Poking around into wild allegations like this could do a lot of damage to good people. You know what I mean?"

Smith couldn't believe that a wild stab like this had actually borne out. "Apparently I do."

"Look, I have to get back to work now. You don't need to call me again unless it's official. I'm sorry, but I have to go now."

"Thanks for your time, Marty. Please tell Ellen I said hello."

The phone had already gone dead in his hand. *Holy shit! Guess I need to make sure the state pension fund isn't invested in Fannie Mae.*

0955 – United Airlines Flight 93

Ziad Jarrah tuned the cockpit VHF omnidirectional rangefinder to the VOR navigational aid at Reagan National Airport, Washington DC. He had also seen the message about the attempted hijackings. He didn't know what attempted hijackings meant, but at least the now knew that other teams were trying to carry out their missions as well.

0956 – Harrisburg, Pennsylvania

Jenny Parrish came back in to the holding room and turned on the television in the corner. CNN came on as Jenny said, "Now it's on TV. Check the crawl line."

Soon after they saw the feed. "*AP report of passenger plane hijacking. Second hijacking attempt: two dead. FAA grounding all aircraft in continental U.S.*"

Detective Smith looked at Graham and asked him, "When they trace the story back to here, do you want to talk to them?"

Elliott had not even thought about it. "What do you think?"

Smith leaned back in his chair. "Well, there is certainly the opportunity to become a celebrity. You might be able to parlay this into a book or maybe even a made-for-TV movie. You can make a few bucks for yourself. If nothing else, you can do the talk show tour for a few weeks if you are interested in that sort of thing. You might even get on the cover of *National Enquirer.*"

Elliott was not very interested in becoming a celebrity, certainly not under these conditions. Besides, what reason did he have to be one? All he had done was wake up thirteen years in the past and he had simply been reacting to events ever since. "But what are they going to say when I say where I came from? They'll all say I'm a nut."

"Maybe, but a nut who was right about today. And you have thirteen more years of predictions to dazzle them with."

"But I don't know how much the future will change, how much I've already changed it. The whole war with Afghanistan and Iraq goes away. At least I guess so. I don't think things as they stand now are going to be enough to justify overthrowing the Taliban. There won't be a Department of Homeland Security, or the Patriot Act. Maybe we won't spend ourselves into bankruptcy, although I'm confident the politicians can come up with plenty of other worthy causes to throw our money at. So the world I know may be gone anyway. Like my family..." *Which probably isn't being helped by thinking about the Laundromat girl.*

Smith was fascinated by the potential future Graham was casually tossing out. War with Iraq and Afghanistan? Another shot at Iraq was fine by him; they should have finished that job ten years ago in his opinion. Afghanistan was a little different. He didn't care for the Taliban any more than the next guy, but they had just been helping that country a few years earlier. It made him wonder how smart it had been to get involved there in the first place. And the Patriot Act? That sounded slightly Orwellian. Smith wanted to come up with something to distract Graham. "I don't know, being wrong doesn't seem to stop all the other professional seers."

Elliott briefly smiled again. "You get my point. I don't want to be a media circus."

"I'm not sure you get that option anymore. Even if I put you out as an anonymous tipster, they'll probably get your name eventually. On the other hand, the public has a pretty short memory. If you lay low, most of them will move on pretty quickly. Since you know so much about President Bush, tell me how he'll do."

"President Bush? You mean as president?"

"Correct."

Elliott recalibrated his mind to think of Bush in the future perfect tense. "He'll do okay I think. I mean, he's barely into his administration when this hits, so he's going to spend the rest of his time in office fighting the Global War on Terror. America demanded action. I didn't agree with all of his decisions, but at least he made them. Then there were other problems that came up."

"Like what?"

"The economy will come unglued. All over the world, not just here. And Hurricane Katrina is going to smash us. Yep, that's another one by the way, somebody needs to tell New Orleans that their levees aren't going to be strong enough to stop the hurricane that's coming through. They have about four years to get them fixed. Otherwise they're going to lose about a thousand people and the whole city will flood. If nothing else, they need to evacuate the city when the hurricane is reported and not mess around. Indonesia will get hit by a tidal wave that kills about a quarter of a million people, too. Japan has a Tsunami coming, but that's about a decade away. It'll flood out the countryside including one of their nuclear reactors."

"I thought you said the future is going to change from what you knew."

"I don't think I'm going to change the weather."

"Well, write all this stuff down and drop it off tomorrow. I'll pass it along to whomever I can get to read it, but I assume there is going to be a great deal of skepticism. Assuming you're still with us tomorrow, of course."

"I'll put it on my to-do list. Does this mean you're going to let me go?"

"Once we run out of terrorists, I don't see much reason to keep you here. I'll have to convince my boss though. And I've been trying to hold them off, but the FBI will probably want to talk to you at some point."

"Good, I really didn't want to go to jail if I could help it. So when the press finally comes around, what are you going to tell them about me?"

Detective Smith had been thinking about that for a while. "For what it's worth, I'll tell them whatever you want me to tell them, sir."

0957 – United Airlines Flight 93

Thomas Burnett again contacted his wife on the air phone. "Tom, is that you?"

"Yes it is, honey. What have you heard?"

"According to the TV, there has been another hijacking attempt. Two of the suspects were killed. The FAA is grounding all the flights in the U.S. Are you okay?"

"Yes, I am. This whole situation is weird. It sounds like these jerks cut up the pilots pretty bad. That doesn't make any sense. Who are they gonna get to fly the plane?"

"I don't know."

Tom thought for a moment and then exclaimed, "Oh my God, it's a suicide mission!"

"Maybe not, just try to blend in, okay?"

"We'll see. I have to go, he's looking at me again. I love you."

0958 – Harrisburg, Pennsylvania

Elliott finally focused on the last sentence in the CNN crawl line. *The FAA is grounding planes anyway!*

"Detective, will you be able to check and see what planes divert into Harrisburg?"

Smith knew the angle Elliott was coming from. "You want to know if your wife's plane will come in here after all? Technically you know there is no reason for me to know that information in order to aid my investigation." It wasn't that the information would be secret, just that he wasn't really supposed to be spending taxpayer time and effort running down leads for a suspect's love life instead of conducting an investigation. Smith laconically thought to himself that on the other hand, without Graham he wouldn't have an investigation in the first place.

"Yeah, I know. It's a favor, not a demand which I am not in a position to make anyway. I just want to know."

Smith looked around and saw that at that moment, Officer Jenny Parrish happened to be back in the room. Smith knew she was a bit of a romantic; her desk always had one of those "Guy-with-his-long-hair-blowing-in-the-wind-despite-being-indoors" books on it. She had clearly been fascinated by Graham's story about his wife and family, and she looked right at Smith as she gave him a small nod. Jenny would be a willing accomplice, and Smith could think of worse crimes to commit. He gave her a small nod back. She smiled and promptly left the room.

"Jenny, I still need that flight manifest." Turning to Graham, he said, "Let's see what happens."

Elliott, who had watched the entire silent exchange, gave him a small smile back.

0959 – American Airlines Flight 394

Tiffany instinctively looked up as the pilot came on over the intercom.

"Folks, this is your captain speaking. I'm sorry, but it looks like we are going to have to land a little early. There is nothing wrong with our plane, but the FAA has directed us to land. Looks like we are going to have to divert into Harrisburg. Unfortunately I don't know for how long, but we'll try and get going again just as quick as we can. Once again, there is nothing wrong with our aircraft, and I do apologize for the inconvenience."

Tiffany was not excited about the change in itinerary. She didn't know anyone in Harrisburg, or anything to do there.

Hopefully they wouldn't be stuck there overnight. *I wonder where I can go in Harrisburg to kill an evening...*

1000 – Flight Alpha Kilo

"Alpha Kilo 1, Ops."

"Go ahead, Ops."

"United Flight 93 just turned on a heading to Washington DC. We also have a tip that DC is their likely final destination."

"Copy. Can a local do an intercept?"

"A flight out of Langley is being scrambled, but they are unarmed."

That's a big help. "Copy. We'll move to intercept, but we won't have enough fuel to get back to Otis. Request permission to divert to Andrews after the intercept."

"Approved. We'll call ahead and let 'em know you're coming. By the way, there was a second hijacking attempt. Two of the attackers were killed without gaining control of the aircraft. Good luck, Alpha Kilo One."

"Thanks, Ops. Chop, it sounds like whoever is doing this is a bunch of fanatics. We need to be ready for anything."

"Two."

1001 – American Airlines Flight 77

Pilot Charles Burlingame took in the FAA grounding order. "American Airlines Flight 77 copies." Then he turned to his first officer and said, "David, please figure out our closest divert airfield and get in touch with them."

"Roger that, Charlie. Why do I have the feeling that that boarding denial we had makes us the luckiest plane in the air today?"

Burlington was glad that it wasn't their day to get taken

hostage by a bunch of crazies. "I think you may be right, partner."

1002 – The Pentagon, Arlington, VA

Max Bielke was part of the human mass stacked around the Pentagon as a result of the directed building evacuation. By now, most of the crowd knew that there had been several hijacking attempts of aircraft in the U.S., and the rumor swirling through the crowd was that the hijackers had taken the planes in order to crash them into buildings in the U.S. That sounded a bit far-fetched to Max. However, if it was true, the two-war veteran thought that putting everyone into an open area made them an even more inviting target. Or what if the supposed hijackers were coordinated with suicide truck bombers who would drive their deadly loads into the exposed crowd? It seemed to Max they would be safer inside the building, or somewhere else. He was just going to locate his boss to suggest that they should disperse when the word came over the loudspeakers:

"Attention, all personnel. For your own safety, all Pentagon employees are instructed to depart the area immediately. Further instructions will be disseminated via your section recall rosters. I say again, all Pentagon employees are to depart the area immediately."

Max sighed to himself as he briefly looked around at his confused fellow coworkers, waved goodbye and started moving home. *So much for today being productive.*

1003 – Harrisburg, Pennsylvania

Graham looked down the list of names on the pages of the eagerly-awaited, freshly-faxed United Flight 93 roster. "Here he is. Todd Beamer. That's your guy. You tell him the situation, he'll do something about it."

Detective Smith couldn't understand why he had to inject into the situation. "Won't he just do something about it anyway?"

"Not now. Remember the family and friends whom the passengers were calling were the ones telling them about the suicide crashes that had already been occurring. The crashes themselves are a game-changer. Without them, Beamer and the people they are talking to will probably assume it's a regular hijacking." What an oxymoron, Elliott thought to himself.

"Okay, Elliott." It was the first time Smith had called Graham by his first name. He took the roster back, circled Beamer's name, and called for Officer Parrish, who was suddenly the most helpful person in the building. "Jenny, get me the cell phone number for this guy immediately, and I'll need a telephone override authority. Actually, get me his wife's home number too. I might have to cut in from that end if he's using an airphone."

"Yessir. Still checking that other thing."

"Thanks." Smith turned back to Graham. "So what else can you tell me about the bad guys?"

"There are four of them. One is trained to fly airplanes but not to land them. Like I've been telling you all along, these guys are fanatics bent on getting to Paradise. The passengers were apparently about to retake control of the aircraft, so the one behind the wheel decided killing a planeload of infidels was better than nothing. He pushed the nose over and tanked it right into a field in the middle of Shanksville."

"Really, here in Pennsylvania?"

"Yep."

"Why Shanksville?" Smith had been through there several times, and couldn't think of anything worth blowing up there.

"It was just where they happened to be at the time the passengers were taking back the airplane. I'm sure the terrorists had never even heard of the place where they died."

Smith thought about that. "So you don't know of any bargaining or blackmailing or threats that will deter him or his team?"

"Now that he has control of the plane, no way. You've seen how hard the other two teams tried to complete their attacks. The only way this ends well is for his limp body to be pried out of the pilot's seat before the plane hits the ground."

1004 – American Airlines Flight 11

Chuck Jones and Jeff Coombs tried to ease the big plane into their final approach to Logan International Airport at 1500 feet altitude. Chuck turned back to look at Carol Bouchard, who was standing uneasily next to the cockpit door.

"It's now or never Carol. See if you can get the pilot revived."

"Okay, Chuck." She turned to John and began shaking him. "John, John, can you hear me? We need your help!'"

Chip Hansen came on the line. "You're coming in hot Flight 11, you need to crack back the throttle to not more than 150 knots and lower your flaps to 20 degrees."

"Not full flaps?"

"That's affirmative Flight 11, you're running on one engine."

"11 copies Tower, I don't want to stall out and I'm already fighting the dead engine."

"Roger, Flight 11, but if you can't stop, you'll overshoot the runway and potentially end up in the water. How are the crew pilots doing?"

"We're trying to revive one, but they were both beat up pretty bad by the hijackers."

"Okay. Lower flaps now."

"John, John, please wake up!"

1005 – United Airlines Flight 93

Mark Bingham was game for whatever the rest of his fellow passengers decided to do to stop their attackers, and was confident that with his six-four, 225 pound frame he could make life miserable for their captors. Mark had played on two national champion rugby teams at Cal-Berkeley, twice defended his long-time boyfriend from attempted muggings, and still proudly displayed the scar he received while running with the bulls in Pamplona, Spain. He had overslept that morning and nearly missed the flight, which seemed like a bad thing at the time, but now he laconically told himself that at least he was well-rested for whatever was to come. He had made a quick call to his mother to tell her he loved her. Now Mark glanced around calmly at the knot of determined-looking men grouped around him figuring out a plan. They were coming to the conclusion that the "bomb" strapped to the waist of one of their hijackers was phony, although just to be sure, they would separate it from him as soon as they could. They also had found a passenger who knew how to fly, although only in single-engine planes, but at least he gave them a chance if they got the plane back. Mark hated to lose, and he sure wasn't going to lay down for these scrawny-looking Hajjis just because they had a couple of knives.

1006 – Harrisburg, Pennsylvania

Elliott's mind was continuing to drift back to the

Laundromat girl, against his better judgment. He thought he recalled that she had abruptly stopped working there about a year later, and the word amongst the block bachelors was that she had gotten married. He had never seen her after that, and probably hadn't thought about her in years, which counterintuitively made her more interesting to him. It gave her an unknown, exotic quality beyond what he might have felt if he had simply run into an old girlfriend.

It also gave him an opportunity to be disingenuous and tell himself that since it would be a year before she was spoken for, anything he did with her would not impact her long-term future either. Thus he would not realistically be jeopardizing any future happiness of hers either.

Besides, how could he cheat on Tiffany if technically they hadn't even met yet? How could he know that their relationship would work this time around, and he wasn't just wasting his time pursuing a dream from another dimension? Why shouldn't he pursue his own happiness given the opportunity?

Just a little investigation couldn't possibly change his future with Tiffany. And after all, it had been a very nice smile…

1007 – Boston, Massachusetts

Marty Jackson toggled the microphone. "WBZ, come in."

"Go ahead, Marty."

"I see the plane coming in now. It's a 767, looks like American. It's probably the one. Are we ready to go live?"

"One minute, Marty."

"Okay. In three it's going to be too late." *C'mon, guys, we aren't going to get a second take.*

1008:30

WBZ tower came back on the radio. "Okay, Marty, you're on in 5, 4, 3..."

"This is Marty Jackson coming to you from the skies above Boston, where a courageous struggle for life is coming to a dramatic conclusion. An American Airlines flight which was reportedly hijacked by terrorists armed with knives and retaken by the passengers is coming in for an emergency landing at Logan Airport. We are flying as close to the restricted flight path as possible and can only watch and pray for the safety of the passengers."

1008:45 – Harrisburg, Pennsylvania

Detective Smith looked at the CNN cutaway. "Here they come."

Elliott Graham recognized the CNN anchor, although again far younger than he remembered. The sound was piped into the room just as she said, "This is Carol Lin. We are getting ready to go live to the skies over Boston, where an American Airlines flight that was hijacked and subsequently recaptured by the passengers is coming in for an emergency landing at Logan International Airport. We are joining the transmission of Marty Jackson of CBS affiliate WBZ of Boston, who is reporting from a traffic helicopter flying just outside the restricted flight path of the emergency aircraft. You are watching their television broadcast."

Graham felt the surrealism of the moment, of the day, at last. Conflicting emotions and questions raced through his mind. What would be the outcome of this day, and how would it affect him? Would he move on to a life where the victims of

9/11 were still alive? Would they want to meet him? Some might, but others might just want to fade back into the woodwork. Would he want to meet them? He wasn't sure, but even if he did, what would he say to them? What could he say to them? No matter what they might think of him, he did not think of himself as a hero. He was just a guy Fate picked to try and change the course of 9/11. They were the heroes. They are *still* the heroes, he quickly corrected himself.

"Good luck, guys," he said softly, almost to himself.

"Amem," chimed in Smith.

1009 – American Airlines Flight 11

American Airlines Flight 11 was passing through 500 feet, and Chuck was having problems keeping the big plane on glide path. The runway was getting bigger and bigger but he kept getting pushed to the right of the glide path. He heard Carol Bouchard still unsuccessfully attempting to revive the pilot.

The radio cracked with the voice of Boston Tower. "Flight 11, you are still coming in too hot. Bring it back more. You're almost down to 400 feet."

"Copy, Tower. I'm trying." He looked over at Jeff who was trying to mirror his movements with the controls. The runway sure looked small with all that water around it. *I don't think we can do this on our own without making a mess* Chuck thought to himself. He could see that Logan International had everything waiting for them next to the airstrip: ambulance, fire, police, even rescue boats in the harbor. *I guess we're gonna need them. Sorry 'bout this folks.*

300 feet.

Chip practically shouted into the microphone, "Flight 11, slow down!"

Chuck was trying, but couldn't figure out how to do it without stalling. Then he heard a detached voice from directly behind him.

"Your glide angle is too steep and you have too much flaps. Push it down a bit more, ease your throttles back and bring the flaps back to twenty percent. And stomp on that rudder like you mean it."

Chuck and Jeff looked back to see a blood-stained Thomas McGuiness leaning unsteadily against the bulkhead door.

Chuck asked, "Do you want to get in here?"

"No time and I can barely stand. Get to work!"

You got it! Chuck turned around and moved the flap lever back. As he reduced the power, he felt the plane settle in smoothly.

150 feet.

"Better, Flight 11, but you're still gonna have to stomp on the brakes when you touch down."

Thomas said, "You're doing fine. Cut speed and push the nose forward just a bit and keep that rudder pressed hard."

They were passing over the landing lights.

Thomas said, "I'm gonna reverse your engines just before we touch down. We're going to need every foot we can get. And come off the rudder to try to straighten out before we hit."

"Got it!" Chuck said.

"Reverse now! Straighten out."

Chuck threw the engines into reverse but was unable to straighten out the rudder before he felt the plane drop and land with a hard thud on the tarmac.

"Brakes now! Turn right!"

Chuck and Jeff stood on the brakes, but the crabbing from fighting the unresponsive engine had caused them to immediately veer to the left.

"Both brakes!"

Chuck tried to compensate but the 767 was quickly onto the grass, which further slowed the aircraft but also tilted it until the left wing dug into the ground, spinning the plane perpendicular to the runway. He could hear the screams from the passengers but immediately sensed that they would be able to get the plane stopped in time. Nonetheless, it seemed like an eternity to Jeff before the plane was rolling to a stop.

"Cut your engine!"

Chuck complied and breathed a sigh of relief, smiling at Jeff as they heard the clapping and shouting from the back of the plane.

Thomas had fallen to his knees during the landing. He simply lay there as he said, "Good job, rookies. Any landing you can walk away from is a good one."

Among the crowd of celebrating passengers and crew, David Angell hugged Lynn and said, "I guess today wasn't our day to die after all."

1010:30 – Logan International Airport, Boston, Massachusetts

Vasily Rostov was personally leading the massive mixed security detail waiting on the ground at Logan Airport for the hatches of American Airlines Flight 11 to pop open so he could climb on board and get his hands on the assholes who had hijacked an airplane from *his* airport to use as a giant flying bomb against America. He wasn't sure if he was going to be happier to find them all dead or if there would still be any alive to question, not that he gave a damn what the hell they were thinking and who they thought they were doing it for.

What a freakin' day! Jose better not be sick tomorrow, that's for damned sure.

1011 – Boston, Massachusetts

Marty Jackson practically shouted into the microphone, like an announcer at a sporting event, "They're down, they're down, they're down!"

Elliott Graham unsuccessfully tried to fight back his tears as he watched the emergency exits open and the inflatable slides deploy. He saw a blonde-haired lady jump onto the slide as an older man with a bandaged hand helped her. The man smiled and waved out the door.

"In all my time flying and broadcasting in the air, that was the most wonderful bad landing I have ever seen!" exclaimed Marty.

Carol Lin came back on saying, "Thank you to Marty Jackson of WBZ for that exciting coverage of this breaking story! The plane appears to be safely down, so we will go to commercial and get you more details on this breaking story. There are also unconfirmed reports that additional hijacking threats may be present and the FAA is moving to ground all U.S. flights."

1011:30 – One World Trade Center

Scoop Esposito glanced over at the floor placard on the stairwell entrance. "50." *You gotta be kidding me.* He was barely over halfway down, and he was already exhausted. On the bright side, he hadn't run into any pregnant women yet.

I think after this I am going to suggest we move our corporate headquarters to a ranch-style building, maybe at most a split-level. I am definitely getting too old for this! What a day!

1012 – United Airlines Flight 93

Todd Beamer was still on the air phone reciting Psalm 23 along with the GTE supervisor whom he had been initially routed to when he suddenly heard the phone crackle and cut off and then a male voice was on the line.

"This is Detective Smith of the Harrisburg Police Department. Is this Todd Beamer?"

Todd was glad to hear the voice of an authority figure. "Yes, it is. Hey, listen, I'm glad you're on the line. I'm on a plane that has been hijacked by some foreign men and…"

"I know, Todd, that's why I cut into your call. You don't have a lot of time. There are probably four of these guys…"

Todd interrupted him. "Three detective, the flight crew saw three."

"No, its four, one of them probably didn't reveal himself until after the passengers and crew were taken out of first class. Listen, they're not ordinary hijackers. I have an excellent tip that your captors intend to crash the airplane into a government building in DC along with them and all of you."

Todd thought hard for a second. *This cop sure knows a lot about these guys.* "Okay, that actually makes sense. These guys are acting really weird. I think they killed the pilots, or at least hurt them pretty badly. One of our passengers is a pilot, and he thinks this whole situation is really weird. We heard that some other planes were being hijacked too. What do you want us to do?" Todd prepared himself mentally for the answer he already knew he was going to hear.

"Todd, it's up to you, but I think that you and the other passengers need to consider trying to retake the airplane from your captors using anything you can get your hands on. I don't think you have much time to make up your minds."

"Okay, I'm on it. A couple of other guys want to help. One hijacker has what looks like a bomb strapped to his waist, but we think it's fake."

Smith had the phone on speaker and glanced up at Graham, who quietly nodded his head. Smith said, "We're pretty sure it's a fake too."

"Okay, any other advice?"

"The one flying the plane, if he thinks he can't get to his target, he'll crash it where he is. You have to kill this guy to stop him."

Todd took a deep breath. "Thanks for the good cheer, Detective."

"I wish I had better news to share with you. You need to get started pretty soon. Get going and good luck Todd."

Todd ended the call, turned to Tom, Jeremy, Mark, and the others gathered around, and said in as loud a whisper as he dared, "Hey, guys, listen up…"

1012:30 – Two World Trade Center

Police Officer Moira Smith was part of the enormous police force from precincts all over the city that had been summoned to the World Trade Center to assist in evacuating the two huge buildings. She figured that it would probably take close to two more hours to get everyone out, even with several hundred officers participating. At least the weather was cooperative. She would have hated to be dealing with this crush of people in the heat of summer. The dispatch office was saying that the building evacuations ordered citywide were related to hijacking attempts of U.S. commercial airliners.

What would hijackings have to do with needing to evacuate

buildings? Kinda sounds like bureaucratic paranoia to me. This is going to end up being a memorable day.

1013 – Harrisburg, Pennsylvania

Detective Smith turned back to Elliott Graham. "That was him. Sounds like you picked the right guy. They're getting ready to try, he was so excited he hung up on me. The military is sending fighters to intercept too. I hope it doesn't come to that, but they have to prevent the worst if they possibly can. All we can do now is wait."

Elliott was still drying his eyes. "Thank you, Detective."

"No, Elliott, thank you. I don't know how terrible this day would have been without you."

Graham said tightly, through clenched teeth. "I do."

"Yeah, I guess you do."

Elliott reflected for a moment and continued talking, almost to himself, "It's hard to describe what this experience will mean to America. I didn't even personally know anyone who died in the attacks, but a day has not gone by since that I haven't thought about it. It's hard not to. The security apparatus alone will be massively expanded throughout the country. More walls and more checkpoints everywhere. There will be searches and wands just about any place people get together; government buildings, ball games, even amusement parks. And forget about airports. You'll need to get there about two hours early just to have a chance of getting to your plane on time. They'll even make you take your shoes off at security."

Smith cut in "Shoes?"

"Yeah, some moron will get a shoe bomb onto a plane. He almost set it off too. Anyway, today is a dividing line in my life, in all our lives, like nothing within recent memory. Almost everything we experience in America will be placed into before 9/11 or after 9/11."

Smith was still trying to process what a shoe bomb could look like when he heard 9/11 and initially drew a blank. "9/11? You mean 9-1-1?"

"No, not the emergency hotline. Today is September 11th, 2001."

Smith thought for a moment. "Oh, I get it. It gets its own nickname?"

"Yep, and just like saying Pearl Harbor, every American will know exactly what you are referencing. So what happens now?"

"I guess we'll give you a ride back to your apartment, or work, if you prefer. I don't know what else to do with you to be honest. The FBI will probably want to grill you pretty hard, but I can probably put them off until tomorrow. You've probably had enough excitement for today. Stay by a phone in case I need to talk to you again. Actually, I was going to ask you the same question."

"I don't have a clue, but I can't picture going back to work today. I probably won't get anything accomplished except getting yelled at by my boss, if I haven't already been fired. Maybe I'll go have a beer instead. Or a few."

"Tell me where you end up and I might join you when I get done here."

Elliott Graham laughed for the first time that day.

Detective Smith was glad to see Graham relaxing; the guy had certainly had a difficult morning doing nothing more than trying to help his fellow Americans, and most would never appreciate the difference he had made. "So what will you do when you wake up tomorrow?"

"I guess that depends on which tomorrow I wake up in."

"What do you mean?"

"Well, I might wake up back in 2014 and find out the world is the same as it was when I went to bed the night before. In that case, I guess I'll just write it off as a very vivid dream, although I admit I'll probably drop by the police station to see if you're working there."

That was an interesting thought. "Tell me I said hello."

"Will do. Even better, give me a personal detail about yourself before I leave and we'll really mess with your head."

And he even has a sense of humor when he gets a chance. "Sounds like fun. And what if you wake up in a new 2014?"

"Well, I guess I'll have to see what has changed. If I'm lucky, I'll wake up next to my wife and the kids will be in the next room. I'll tell her what a weird dream I had and then go get ready for work. Maybe I will wake up and find I have a different wife, different kids, a different house and maybe even job. If so, I guess that will be my life, although I don't see how she could be better than Tiffany. If I am still a swinging single, I guess I will look up Tiffany and see if she is available and interested in getting to know me, but I doubt she will be available."

"You mentioned what you'll do if you wake up tomorrow, sorry, my tomorrow. But what if tomorrow is today again?" Detective Smith was starting to confuse himself too.

"You mean, assuming I remember this day. Maybe I just keep waking up in this day every morning with no prior knowledge, and end up spending the day sitting in this holding room. Maybe I already have been doing this. For all I know, this could be my thousandth time going through this day. It sounds weird, but after all that has happened today the weird is becoming routine."

Which would make it Smith's thousandth time going

through the day too. Too bad, his heartburn was starting to kick in. "Okay, so assuming you remember going through this version of today the next time, then what will you do differently the next time around, just out of curiosity? Have you learned anything about stopping hijackers?"

"So in other words, let's assume that I wake up on September 11th again, but remembering everything that happened today. I'll get going a little bit sooner for starters. It took me about half an hour to understand where I was this morning, or more precisely *when* I was, and to start taking some real action. Then when I start calling people I need to keep it to one call per telephone tops. I'll know what I want to say before I get the people on the line so that I stay at a minute of conversation when I get an authority on the line. I won't waste a lot of time arguing with the person on the other end. I'll just make my point and hang up since you guys record the whole conversation anyway. If I remember everything from today, it will help that now I know the flight numbers and departure locations of the affected aircraft. I'll probably use my car so I can be more mobile, although I'll also need to be prepared to walk away from it at some point and proceed on foot. Not forgetting my wallet when I go rushing out the door would probably be a good idea too. Eventually I'll just head for the police station."

Smith was impressed. Not bad analysis by Graham of his first foray into borderline criminal activity. "Anything else?"

"Not to sound like a Hallmark moment, but as soon as the police pick me up, I'll know to ask to speak to you."

"You guys have Hallmark?"

Elliott started to rise up in his chair, but saw Smith smiling at him.

"Gotcha."

1014 – United Airlines Flight 93

Thomas Burnett had gotten through to his wife again, who was still trying to convince him to be unobtrusive.

"If you sit quietly, they probably will leave you alone."

Burnett wanted to believe his wife, but unfortunately he didn't. "I don't think so, honey. Another passenger had a policeman cut into his call to tell him the FBI has a tip that these guys are going to crash the planes. I told you these guys have been acting weird. They aren't trying very hard to stop us from making these calls. Some of us are getting ready to try and retake the plane from these assholes. I don't think we have much choice now. Gotta go. Don't worry, we're going to do something. I love you."

"I love you too," she responded into the disconnected line.

1844:30
(1014:30 Eastern Standard Time) – Afghanistan

Hajji Ebrahim steeled himself as he prepared to walk into the room where The Leader was completing his prayers.

The Jihad against the West had taken the loose organization known as al-Qaeda (The Base) across a wide swath of the Muslim world, from Pakistan and Sudan, throughout the Arabian Peninsula and back to their current location in Afghanistan. Founded as the successful campaign against the Soviet Union in Afghanistan was concluding, the organization was a religious movement combined with an army of operatives who would wage global war in support of their goal of a Caliphate that would unite the Muslim world under their vision of the pure Islam practiced in the early days of the umma (community of believers). The organization had seen its share of success, proven by the fact that they were currently denounced as a terrorist organization by the United Nations, the European Union, and the target they considered the greatest threat to the resurgence of Sunni Islam, the United States. Their mujahedeen had made high-profile attacks against U.S. embassies in Africa, then seriously damaged a U.S. warship in Yemen. These successes led to increased U.S. pressure on the organization and had driven them back to their old hunting grounds in Afghanistan. They were willing to accept this short-term inconvenience. It meshed with their strategy of exhausting the Dar al-Harb (House of War) in a long war of attrition that targeted non-believers, including what they viewed as "impure" sects of Islam and even women and children.

The organization had been planning what was referred to as "the planes" operation for two years. The Leader had great faith in its potential for success, and saw it as a means to take the fight straight to the heart of Dar al-Harb and inspire fear and respect for their power among the enemies of true Islam. Target possibilities such as nuclear power plants had been nominated but rejected in favor of high-profile buildings that they felt symbolized the corruption and brutality of the capitalist, imperialist, Christian world. Mujahedeen familiar with the West and its languages had been carefully selected and funded, then sent for the training needed to carry out their missions. The key operatives, the pilots, ironically received their training at schools in the U.S., right under the very noses of their intended victims. Despite setbacks, the operation had moved forward until it was ready for execution.

Ebrahim knew that The Leader was excited about the timing of the operation. "Excited" was a relative term, for The Leader was actually a very soft-spoken person not given to displays of emotion. Even while being exposed to artillery or missile bombardment against the Russians in Afghanistan, he had been renowned for remaining calm and composed. He was shy and usually wore a slight smile, although he seldom laughed. His terseness did not prevent him from appreciating the importance of information in advancing the global Jihad. He maintained a media team to monitor important news agency broadcasting. Although he usually lived in homes or other buildings, he liked to record his video messages in one of the caves dotting Afghanistan to evoke the image of the struggles of the early Umma and the Prophet Mohammad (Peace Be Upon Him).

All of the al-Qaeda members who knew of the impending planes operation were excited too. They needed a victory to regain their standing with their Taliban hosts. Only two days earlier, the Taliban had executed a brilliant operation when a suicide team disguised as a news crew had succeeded in blowing themselves up along with Ahmed Shah Massoud, the formidable leader of the Northern Alliance coalition of disparate warlords still clinging to a fragment of Afghanistan's rugged mountains. His demise was expected to effectively end the resistance to Taliban control of all Afghanistan. Bereft of the only leader capable of unifying them, the remaining warlords would flee or submit to the Taliban. Their hosts were giddy to the point of insufferableness, and Ebrahim was sure he was not the only member of al-Qaeda who had eagerly looked forward to a successful outcome to "the planes" operation as a way to return them to their former stature versus their Taliban counterparts, who in his opinion lacked the global perspective of al-Qaeda.

Ebrahim did not want to go inside, but he knew that The

Leader did not like to be put off. He slowly opened the door to find The Leader in the middle of the room.

"Ahlan ya Osama."

Osama bin Laden glanced up from his kneeling position on the small prayer rug he used with his usual slight smiling expression. "Ahlan ya Ebrahim."

"The news of the airplanes operation is beginning to be broadcast by the world press."

Ebrahim saw The Leader continue to gaze at him with the same expression. He suspected that The Leader already knew what he was going to say. He continued on.

"Two of the mujahedeen teams are reported to have tried to carry out their missions. Information is still very sketchy at this time."

The Leader continued to stare silently back at him. The unspoken *And?* filled the short distance between them like a widening chasm of tension. Ebrahim felt his face flush as he spoke again.

"The reports indicate that the teams were not successful in reaching their targets, or crashing their planes into the ground. We do not know how the infidels were able to stop them."

The same even expression looked back at him. *And?* Ebrahim would have been more comfortable if The Leader were yelling or throwing things.

"There is still no information about the other two teams. Perhaps they will have better luck," Ebrahim added impulsively and immediately regretted. A mistake on his part, betraying his disappointment and emotion to The Leader.

Still no reaction from The Leader.

Ebrahim regained his self-control and continued, "The Americans are bound to trace the attacks back to us and attempt to strike with their remote missiles as they have done in the past. It is no longer safe for you here. We must begin preparations to leave immediately."

After several seconds, The Leader nodded ever so slightly in return.

Ebrahim had neither purpose nor desire to remain in the room any longer.

"My apologies for disturbing your prayers, Effendi."

Osama responded in a soft, even tone. "Shukran (thank you) Ya Ebrahim."

Ebrahim backed slowly out of the room and turned to close the door. He glanced back in the room just before the door closed, seeing The Leader with his hands clasped in front of his face in prayer as his tall, lean frame began to sink to the rug underneath him.

1015 – United Airlines Flight 93

Todd Beamer felt a sense of calm come over him now that they had made the decision to try and retake their airplane. Most of them, anyway. A few of the passengers on the plane still thought that they should not attempt to interfere with their hijackers even after he had passed on his conversation with the police detective. Others were simply paralyzed with fear, mumbling on their cell phones or crying to themselves. Todd couldn't understand how a person could not even try to save themselves, and just do nothing but sit and hope. No matter. They didn't need everyone to successfully retake the plane, just enough of them. He thought he had found some guys who looked like they were capable of action and wanted to help get their plane back. In fact, he figured the rugby guy Mark and the judo guy Jeremy could probably retake the plane all by themselves. One of the flights attendants was even a former policewoman, and looked like she couldn't wait to get after these guys. If he thought there was a better option he would have been more than willing to try it, but that policeman sounded pretty sure of his information, and it jived with Todd's conclusions about the hijackers' intentions. Better to try and do something than just sit around waiting for the end. They had gathered up whatever weapons they could find and could see their hijackers were getting nervous. The biggest problem was trying to hold back the guy who said he could fly; it wasn't going to do any good to pull off this miracle if their only pilot option got himself stabbed before he could get the plane down safely. He looked around one more time at the gathering clump of passengers and crew who were edging forward, ready to rush the hijackers. "Are you guys ready? Let's roll."

1016

Jarrah was distracted from flying the aircraft as he heard commotion coming from the back of United Flight 93 and quickly turned to Saeed. "Is there something? A fight?" Al-Ghamdi was already up and moving through the cockpit door toward the back of the aircraft.

1017

As al-Ghamdi opened United Flight 93's cockpit door and stepped out, he saw that Ahmed al-Nami and Ahmed al-Haznawi were being overwhelmed by a dense phalanx of shouting passengers using sheer mass as their primary weapon, while also throwing anything they had found in the back of the plane. He knew they should not have let the aircrew go into the galley unobserved, but they only had four hijackers and couldn't really control the crowd. *Damned American border security.* Al-Nami was already down in the aisle with two burly passengers and a black female flight attendant kicking him mercilessly. al-Haznawi was still on his feet but was losing ground to the attackers and would shortly be in the crosswalk, if the passengers overwhelming al-Nami didn't clamber over the seats and get behind him first. Obviously the passengers did not believe the bomb threat. Al-Ghamdi knew that there was nothing he could do to save his fellow mujahedeen in the cabin of the aircraft from being overrun, quickly turned around and ran back to the cockpit.

Even before Saeed Al-Ghamdi reappeared in the cockpit, the sound outside had already told Jarrah what was happening. The passengers were trying to retake the airplane and probably would, given enough time. But all they needed to do was hold off the passengers for a few more minutes and he and his brother mujahadeen would be able to complete their mission. He turned and yelled to Saeed "They want to get in here. Hold, hold from the inside. Hold from the inside. Hold!" Al-Ghamdi nodded, moved into the cockpit, locked the door and prepared to hold the passengers off, instinctively turning his feet as if digging into soft ground.

The mujahadeen had one big advantage, control of the plane. Jarrah tried to buy time for himself and the mujahedeen in the cabin struggling against the passengers by pitching the nose of the aircraft up and down.

1018 – Flight Alpha Kilo

Chop saw the 757 in the distance.

"Tallyho, Lead, target at one o'clock low."

"I got 'em, Chop. Follow me in."

"Two."

1019 – United Airlines Flight 93

Jarrah stabilized United Flight 93 after conducting a series of abrupt maneuvers accompanied by screaming from the back of the airplane and turned back toward Saeed.

"Is that it? Shall we finish it off?"

Saeed responded, "No. Not yet. When they all come, we finish it off." But both men knew they didn't have much time.

Reassured by Saeed, Jarrah refused to let himself be distracted by sympathizing with his fellow hijackers and the losing fight they were enduring in the rear of the airplane against the infidels, even though these men were his friends and comrades who had all been preparing for this mission together for a long time. That was what they were there for, they had all willingly volunteered to be at the forefront of this great campaign to demonstrate the glory and power of Allah to the unbelievers, and it only meant that they would get to Paradise a few minutes before he did, where their reward for their courage in fulfilling His will would be awaiting them.

1019:30 – Flight Alpha Kilo

Chop said, "Lead, do you see that?" They're bobbing and weaving all over the place. What do you think is going on in there?"

Lizard instinctively knew. "The pax are probably trying to retake the aircraft. The hijackers are trying to disrupt them. This is going to happen really fast Chop, we probably won't have time for another pass. I'm going to launch missiles, then fire one long cannon burst. Be ready to roll directly into lead and commence firing as soon as I finish firing and roll out."

Lizard wasn't worried about missing an aircraft that size at the short distance they were from the 757, he just wasn't sure his missiles and bullets would be powerful enough to finish off the big plane before it could reach the hijacker's target. *Kamikazes*, he corrected himself.

"Over the city, Lizard?" Chop was unhappy enough to have to shoot a plane full of passengers, it was even worse to think of the wreckage going down in a heavily populated area. Still, he was annoyed at himself for blurting that out. Of course Lizard knew where they were, and knew that they were there to do a job, like it or not.

Lizard knew what Chop was thinking and wasn't happy with the thought either, but the priority was preventing the possibility of a kamikaze crash. "Ops, Alpha Kilo 1."

"Go ahead, Alpha Kilo 1."

"We're over the city, moving into position directly behind the target. The target is bouncing all over the sky."

"Roger. We're being told that the passengers are assaulting the cockpit."

"Copy. I'll call when we are in position. Are we authorized to shoot?" Lizard didn't like the idea of performing a shoot down in the city either, but they had to assume it was preferable to the alternative of letting the terrorists proceed to their intended target, if they were in fact suicides.

"We're working on that Alpha Kilo 1. Maintain current intercept."

1020 – United Airlines Flight 93

As Ziad Jarrah descended through one thousand feet, he looked out United Flight 93's window and saw the taunting, familiar obelisk of the Washington Monument. Three more minutes and Allah's glorious will would be fulfilled right in the heart of the Dar al-Harb. But could they hold on for such a long time? Ziad Jarrah heard the commotion as the passengers attempted to retake the aircraft by hurling plates which were shattering against the walls and hull of the aircraft. He also heard the shouts of the passengers.

"In the cockpit. If we don't, we'll die!"

"Roll it!"

Shortly after, there came what was clearly the sound of the food cart being used by the passengers and crew as a battering ram against the outside of the cockpit door to break it down and force their way inside. Clearly, neither of the Ahmeds were maintaining the struggle against the infidels any longer. Jarrah had been prepared to dive the aircraft straight into the ground if he felt the passengers were about to retake the aircraft, but they were so close to the target that he could actually see it beckoning to him. It would be a greater victory for them if he could get the aircraft to the planned target. Surely Allah would not allow them to get this close to success only to fail. He continued to recite the takbir aloud as he decided he would continue flying the plane to their intended target until the last possible second.

1021 – Flight Alpha Kilo

Lizard continued to decelerate the F-15 as he rolled his aircraft into attack position, leveling off into easy firing position directly behind the big airliner with Chop lined up on his wing. The violent maneuvering being done by the hijackers might be disrupting the passengers and crew assaulting the cockpit, but it wouldn't even begin to allow the passenger plane to avoid air-to-air missiles or cannon fire. All three aircraft were now approaching the heart of DC. As he toggled the microphone, Lizard tried to concentrate as he began a transmission he had trained all his adult life for and hoped he would never have to make.

"Ops, Alpha Kilo 1 in position, requesting permission to fire."

After a few seconds of no reaction, Lizard thought, *What the hell are they waiting for? We're going to lose the shot.*

"I say again, Alpha Kilo 1 in position, requesting permission to fire."

"Stand by Alpha Kilo 1."

Lizard continued to track the airliner as he flew over the familiar buildings of DC, amazed at how the passing seconds of silence seemed more like ages. Finally he lost patience. "Ops, Alpha Kilo 1 in position, requesting permission to fire."

This time the response came back "Alpha Kilo 1, you are cleared to engage. I say again, you are cleared to engage."

About time, thought Lizard. "Copy Ops, Alpha Kilo 1 out. Chop?"

"Two."

Lizard refocused on the large passenger plane bobbing in front of him, toggled the firing button from safe, and prepared to fire.

2132 – Harrisburg, Pennsylvania

Elliott realized he made a mistake after the Harrisburg Police had finally dropped him off at his apartment building.

He had been relieved to learn via Officer Parrish that Tiffany's plane had been diverted to Harrisburg again, and eventually that all planes were being grounded for the remainder of the day, so in all likelihood he would be able to find her right where they first met. But the battle inside him had continued throughout the day; recovering the family he knew versus the excitement of the unknown. Before he really knew what he was doing, he found himself walking around the corner and down the street toward the Laundromat. As he walked by without stopping, he saw the pretty girl standing behind the counter waiting on the only customer in the store. He crossed over to the other side of the street and walked up to the end and back until the customer left the Laundromat. He felt his legs carrying him across the street to the glass door, where he watched his detached hand push the door open, setting the overhead bell ringing. She was working underneath the counter and stood up just as he got there. A confused smile was followed by an awkward silence until Elliott introduced himself to her. He mumbled something about needing change as he remembered he still didn't have his wallet and clumsily shifted to some small conversation, to which she surprised him by pleasantly responding.

She's interested in me. Elliott was gaining confidence as he started asking her when she would be done working. As he did, the store clock began gently chiming the hour. As he glanced at a wall calendar behind her, he saw the face of Tiffany staring back at him. It was a sad face filled with emptiness.

No. The features of her face slowly began to fade and run together.

No! What have I done? The face had turned into a black hole that was expanding to engulf first the calendar, then the wall, then began reaching around the walls of the store to cut him off from his world. Even the floor underneath him began shifting and moving to form a vortex dragging him down.

Tiffany, I'm sorry!

Just as abruptly, the chiming stopped and he found himself staring at the pastel print of a calendar model. Elliott felt soaked in sweat. He immediately turned and staggered out of the Laundromat, leaving a confused and now disappointed girl staring after him.

When he walked into his apartment, he found seven messages waiting on his answering machine. Four were from his department head with each sounding more irritated than the previous one, two from his mother, and one from the local newspaper (those guys *were* good at their job). He unwound himself on his couch and stared at the news coverage which was more or less dedicated to reporting or commenting on the events of the day until he finally turned off the television.

All Elliott had eaten that day was his hasty breakfast and a candy bar from the police department vending machine. He was ravenously hungry, yet barely even noticed as he finally got up and started getting ready. He stood in front of his closet for twenty minutes trying to decide which shirt to wear. Should he wear the red-and-brown striped one he actually wore the first time he had lived this day, or should he wear the solid blue shirt Tiffany always complimented him on when she saw him in it? It wasn't that he had such a great memory for his dress that night that allowed him to ponder this issue, it was simply that they were the only two collared shirts he had found in his apartment that didn't have a logo of a sports team or bar on them. *What did she see in him anyway?* Should he try to replicate that night as much as possible, or take a small step to try and improve his odds? He could bring both, make an on-the-spot decision at the bar, and throw the other one away. A forty-dollar shirt seemed like small potatoes next to the rest of his life. He switched between them three times before he realized he was simply stalling, put on the red-and-brown, and strode down to his car.

He drove himself to the bar to avoid running into anyone else he knew. He wanted no more chance encounters or conversations that could distract him or change his trajectory. He barely acknowledged his landlady as he walked by leaving the apartment building. He had not returned any of his phone messages, although it had been soothing to hear his mother's voice. His mind was finally focused on the right person, and he wanted it to stay that way.

Elliott arrived at the restaurant, where he slowly circled until he determined that he could not observe the bar area from the outside of the building. He parked his car, got out and walked on unsteady legs into the foyer, where he stood until another group of patrons left the restaurant. As they did, he peered inside and scanned the bar area. There she was, right where she had been the first time they had been there! He thought she still looked gorgeous in 2014, but was amazed how much more so she looked this evening.

He was still staring when he felt like he was being awakened from a dream as someone shouted his name again, this time grabbing and shaking his arm as well.

"Hey, Elliott!"

It was gregarious Devin Gardiner from the History Department. Devin had gotten married and moved on from the college in 2008 and their families still exchanged Christmas cards, although Elliott had not seen him since he left. Elliott had forgotten that his fellow teaching assistants would probably be here tonight as well, since that was the group he had been with on his first 9/11. Like a rushing flood, he realized he had not wanted to start a conversation with someone who knew him because he feared that it might trigger the end of whatever life he was living through. He stared at Devin uncomprehendingly as he rambled on.

"Elliott, are you all right? Where have you been? Dude, Dr. Forbes is mega-pissed at you. Where were you today? No calls, nothing. Consuela had to cover your classes. Have you seen the news? Hey man, are you even listening to me? You look like you're in outer space or something. We're all over there, come on over."

Elliott glanced along his outstretched hand to the table filled with his friends from the college, who were smiling and gesturing for him to join them.

Not now. Elliott knew he had to give him something, and actually he did want to get caught up (in a sense) with old friends, some of whom he had not seen for years. "Thanks Devin, there's something I need to do right now. Save a spot for me, okay?"

Devin wasn't that easy to put off. "Just have a drink first, everyone is worried about you man. Are you okay, did something happen? Are you coming in tomorrow?"

"I'll come back in a few minutes, okay? Just order my usual for me." *What was my usual in 2001? Did I have one? I hope he knows.*

"Come pour it yourself, man. What's so important you can't come over?"

What the heck. "I want to go talk to the brunette over at the bar first."

"Seriously? Usually you need at least two beers before you go talk to a chick."

"I've had my eye on her for some time."

"Are you kidding? You just walked in. Besides, Larry already took a shot. She wasn't very interested in him."

Yeah, and he'll still be trying ten years from now, and she still won't like him. "I'm going to go talk to her anyway. I'll come over later, okay?"

Devin recoiled slightly as Elliott's tone changed in the last sentence. "Dude, relax. We're just worried about you, that's all. If she's that important to you, go for it. Besides…" Devin's voice trailed off as he glanced behind Elliott "…she's not there anyway."

Elliott spun around. "What? No!" He had not meant to be that abrupt to his old friend, but this was what he had feared. *Where was she?* This was probably his punishment for talking to the Laundromat girl. He tuned out the still-talking Devin as he moved to the empty seat where Tiffany had been and looked around, but didn't see her. He tried to flag down the bartender to ask if he knew where she had gone. He was searching intently around the room, and swore that the girl in the corner motioning behind him with her eyes looked like the police officer from the station, Jenny. Suddenly, his racing heart skipped a beat as the familiar lilac scent filled his face while a feminine arm reached by him to place a tip on the bar. He turned and felt his blood drain as he gazed less than a foot into Tiffany's eyes. She viewed him with a mixture of concern and curiosity. Elliott was at an absolute loss for words.

Tiffany finally broke the silence. "Are you okay?" Her hand brushed her hair back as she turned ever so slightly towards him and he saw the familiar coy smile that still made him melt.

"Yes, I am."

CHAPTER TWO

---///---

0600 – Harrisburg, Pennsylvania

Elliott Graham woke up in an empty bed.

Was that lilac he smelled?

GLOSSARY

Ahlan – Hello (Arabic)

Auger in – Crash

Dar al Harb – House of War: all parts of the world not under Islamic sovereign control (Arabic)

Effendi – Lord, master (Turkic)

FAA – Federal Aviation Administration

FCOC – Facility Calls Operation Center

FUBAR – Fouled Up Beyond All Recognition (approximately)

Hajji – A Muslim who has completed the pilgrimage to Mecca (Arabic)

In Sha Allah – God wills it (Arabic)

KY-58 – A secure voice radio unit utilized by US military aircraft

LNO - Liaison officer

Mujahedeen – Warriors (Arabic)

NEADS – Northeast Air Defense Sector

Ops – Operations

Pashtun – Afghan tribe

Pax – Passengers

Sayeret Matkal – General Staff Reconnaissance Unit (Hebrew)

Shukran – Thank you (Arabic)

Takbir – Muslim prayer: "God is Great" (Arabic)

Umma – Community of Muslims (Arabic)

VHF - Very high frequency

VOR - VHF Omni-directional radio range

Wahhabi – A conservative branch of Sunni Islam

WMD – Weapons of Mass Destruction

Ya – Oh; sir (Arabic)

Yallah – By Allah; hey (Arabic)